Jaid Black

Lost In Trek

The Definitive Guide to the Trek Mi Q'an Universe

ELLORA'S CAVE
ROMANTICA PUBLISHING

An Ellora's Cave Romantica Publication

www.ellorascave.com

Lost in Trek

ISBN 9781419956393
ALL RIGHTS RESERVED.
Lost In Trek Copyright © 2007 Jaid Black
Dementia Copyright © 2002 Jaid Black
Never a Slave Copyright © 2007 Jaid Black
Edited by Nicholas Conrad
Cover art by Darrell King

Trade paperback Publication May 2006

Excerpt from *Death Row* Copyright © Jaid Black, 2004

Also by Jaid Black

❧

About the Author

හ

USA Today bestselling author Jaid Black is the owner and founder of Ellora's Cave Publishing. Recognizing and legitimizing female sexuality as an entity unique from male sexuality is her passion. Jaid has been featured in every available media, from major newspapers like the Cleveland Plain Dealer, to various radio programs, to an appearance on the Montel Williams Show. Her books have received numerous distinctions, including a nomination for Nerve magazine's Henry Miller award for the best literary sex scene published in the English language.

Jaid welcomes comments from readers. You can find her website and email address on her author bio page at www.ellorascave.com.

Tell Us What You Think

We appreciate hearing reader opinions about our books. You can email us at Comments@EllorasCave.com.

LOST IN TREK

ℰℴ

DEMENTIA

ഔ

Chapter One

The highlander jungle of planet Dementia
Kabka star system of the third dimension

ꙮ

Her friends called her the Schemer, or Scheme for short, for she had always been well known for her ability to get out of tight situations. But as she ran through the dense Dementian jungle panting for air, her heartbeat drumming like mad against her chest, Delores Ellison was afraid that, for the very first time in her twenty-nine years, she had gotten herself into a situation there was no squeezing out of.

Her father had always said she was too much like her mother for his peace of mind. Perhaps he had been right.

Dee dashed through the overgrown jungle as fast as her feet would carry her. She ignored the rogue strands of golden hair that whipped into her eyes and stung them, and instead concentrated her energy on escaping the gorilla fighter whose hunting skills were proving to be frighteningly keen.

He's gaining on me, she thought hysterically as she braved a quick glance over her shoulder. *Good God in heaven, do not let this beast enslave me!*

She still didn't know how it had happened, still had no clue how she'd ever been catapulted from Earth to this…this…place. But she had been in Dementia for over a year now and, at least until this night of reckoning, had managed to thwart any would-be slave traders from capturing her.

She had survived on berries and an odd blue fish for sustenance, slept in hollowed out stone caves for protection from the elements, all the while searching in vain for the bizarre stone icon shaped like a gorilla's head that she had been holding when she'd been mystically transported to this dark, frightening world so reminiscent of *Planet of the Apes*. Dee was certain that if only she could find that talisman—or whatever in the hell it was—she could go back to Earth, back to home.

She ran into the night, dashed through the highlander jungle terrain she had grown accustomed to, her breath coming out in short gasps. She knew—*knew*—that the gorilla fighter was gaining on her, would catch her at any moment if she didn't figure out a way to escape him. She could sense his sharp green eyes on her, could hear the low growl of a predator hissing in his throat...

Please, she silently begged the heavens. *I do not want to be a slave! Oh God—oh please God help me!*

Dee ran impossibly faster, ignoring the buzzing sound of the insect predators that swarmed throughout the dense terrain. She knew what those gorillas had done to that one human girl, the one she had tried to escape Dementia with six months ago. Knew too that the Dementian males coveted humanoid females as nothing more than sex slaves and serving girls.

The one tracking her now was called Zaab—General Zaab if she'd overheard the villagers of the Mantus Hoard correctly. Zaab had once been a lowlander lieutenant, but had taken over the highlander Mantus Hoard by force when its elderly leader was assassinated by fellow tribesmen. And so now the new general ruled with an iron fist, and in just under a year had made the Mantus the most respected — and feared — gorilla fighters on the planet.

Zaab. This wasn't the first time he had hunted Dee, not the first time he had attempted to enslave her. But, she thought as she ran faster and faster still, it might well be the last time he'd have to hunt her if she didn't figure a way out of this mess. Twice before he had stalked her, twice before she had thwarted him. The third time would prove to be a charm — but whether for her or for him...

Zaab.

He stood upright like a human, possessed the mental acuity of a human, and even carried the masculine scent of a human, yet this male was no human...

A gorilla. If she didn't get herself out of this situation, Dee thought in anguish as she struggled to breathe, then she would become the sex slave of a gorilla.

No.

The eerily moaning wind swarmed about her, crashing through the rough alien terrain. She could feel him getting close, then closer still, could sense his sharp, possessive eyes narrowed on her...

Run, Dee! Run!

Dee cried out softly in her throat as the low growling sound grew alarmingly closer. Her heartbeat was thumping like a rock against her chest, her blue eyes wide and her breathing labored. She made a quick left turn into the thickest portion of the jungle and dashed into it, knowing it was an unsafe place to be, but also realizing that if she was to thwart Zaab for a third time then this was the only way.

Help me! she mentally pleaded. *Dear God in heaven please help me!*

Dee screamed out when the sharp stinger of a predatorial vine shot through her thigh, effectively throwing her to the ground while it slowly drugged her with hallucinogen. She cried out again when the thick leafy tentacles entwined themselves around her limbs, the snappers instantly shredding what clothing she'd had on as they laid her out spread-eagle and naked on the jungle floor.

Not the vines—oh no, not the vines.

She knew it was over. Knew too that Zaab had won. If the general didn't track her down by scent, then the vines would have their wicked way with her, dining on her cunt juice until she died, dehydrated and mentally broken. Either way, it was over…

The vines were the method Dementians used to break human female slaves to their bidding. The predatorial plant would intravenously pump a euphoric hallucinogen into her system, making her orgasm over and over again, providing them with the juice they dined on, until she literally died of pleasure and dehydration. The hallucinogen would also drive her insane if given too much of it, insuring that the only way she'd ever again possess the mental wherewithal to leave Dementia was through death.

Dee cried out softly as two pink flower buds from the vine clamped onto her nipples and began suctioning at them. They stiffened immediately, causing her to moan. *It's over,* she thought, closing her eyes as the hallucinogen began to take effect. *It's all over...*

The sound of a low, arrogant growl filled her mind. She blinked slowly, opening her blue eyes on a moan as a third flower bud clamped onto her clit and began suctioning it. She shuddered, knowing an orgasm was imminent.

The general stood above her, his piercing green eyes flicking possessively over her naked, splayed-out body. His gaze settled on her cunt and lingered there, then darted up the length of her to meet her eyes.

Zaab.

Dee swallowed roughly, wondering through the euphoric daze that was quickly engulfing her just how long it would take before she was begging the bastard to fuck her. A male in his prime, an alpha male who owned more slaves than she could count, would know very well—too well—how to use the vines to get what he wanted.

She groaned and simultaneously arched her hips as the first powerful orgasm hit. She closed her eyes tightly, not wanting to watch his expression, for she could sense his arrogant pleasure as though it was a tangible thing. He knew he'd won, knew too that he could do anything he wanted with her.

The rustling sound of discarded leather clothing induced her eyes to sleepily open for a moment. It was hard to focus on any one thing for the euphoria was hitting fast, but she was alert enough to recognize the naked, powerful Dementian male standing over her.

Zaab.

His body was at least seven feet tall—probably more. His musculature was extreme, without a doubt the most powerful and heavily-muscled body she'd ever laid eyes on. Two deadly incisors jutted out from his otherwise human-looking teeth, a grim reminder that he could slice through her jugular like melted butter.

Her eyes flicked down to his stone-hard cock. She nervously wetted her lips, again wondering how long it would take before she was begging the general to fuck her.

And then the euphoria kicked in and she no longer cared.

Chapter Two

ဆ

Surreality engulfed all of her senses. Her mind swam as if dreaming, or as if existing on another plane far removed from the cold jungle floor she lay naked and spread-eagle upon. She shuddered and moaned as the flower buds on the vines clamped down harder onto her erect nipples and swollen clit, her legs shaking as she violently climaxed. Again.

And still, the general made no move to fuck her.

She felt like she'd been coming for hours—days even. Yet realistically she knew it was the hallucinogen making her feel that way. No more than fifteen minutes could have passed since the vines had snagged her, but the painfully hedonistic euphoria made the time seem endless.

She needed to be mounted. She needed to be fucked more than she needed to breathe.

Zaab was watching her, she knew. His piercing green eyes were evaluating and assessing her bodily responses with the acuity of a hawk, and yet he still hadn't bothered to touch her, let alone to impale her with his huge cock.

She gritted her teeth, refusing to beg. He knew what the vines were doing to her, realized that she would give anything—do anything—say anything—to be fucked over and over, again and again...

"How do you feel, lass?" he murmured, squatting down beside her on his powerful thighs. He ran a large, rough hand over her belly, then brought it up to cup one breast. Apparently irritated that the suctioning flower bud was in the way of his touching her nipple, he pulled it off, snapped the head and threw that particular portion of the vine to the wayside. He ran his thumb over her nipple, making her gasp, then asked again, "How do you feel?"

Dee wetted her lips, trying to make eye contact but in too dreamy of a state to focus her attention. "I...I...tired," she whispered, closing her eyes again. "Frustrated." That small admission was as close to begging as she'd allow herself to sink.

"Tell me what you need," he murmured. She heard the other flower bud make a popping sound as it was forced from her other nipple. A second later that one was snapped too and two large Dementian hands settled in at her breasts and toyed with her nipples, making them ache so much more than the vines had.

"Please," she whimpered, her hips arching up as much as they could while being roped down to the ground with vines. "Make it stop." Another small admission, but one she couldn't seem to keep from making.

"Hmm," he purred noncommittally, his primal male face coming into her line of vision. His thumbs and forefingers plucked at her nipples, plumping them up.

She sucked in her breath and arched her hips as he settled himself intimately between her outspread thighs. He made no move to displace the flower bud sucking vigorously at her clit, opting instead to watch as she convulsed again from another orgasm the plant-mouth brought on.

"Please," she said more forcefully, refusing to allow her voice to quiver into a pleading sound. "Please."

Zaab ignored her. She gritted her teeth.

The general released her breasts and placed some bizarre, fleshy-looking contraption next to her body, a boxy device she'd never seen before. He removed the needle that the predatorial vine had shot into her thigh and momentarily disabled it by sticking the needled portion of it into the faux flesh-box.

So that was how he would keep the vine alive if he needed it again, she thought hesitantly. He was nobody's fool. He'd disallow the hallucinogen to kill her, but he'd also keep it handy if he needed to torture her into submission with the euphoria it generated.

Good God, she'd never escape him.

Not that the sexual euphoria she was already experiencing was even close to waning, she thought with near hysteria. It seemed to grow worse and worse, making her want to clamp her legs together and squeeze, inducing her breathing to hitch and her pupils to dilate. "Please," she said pitifully, no longer caring if she begged or not. "Please help me."

Zaab purred at her submissive words, his warm palms running over her belly. "I've the feeling you will be worth the wait, lass," he murmured, those piercing green eyes straying down to her puffed-up cunt. She knew he was referring to the other two times she'd escaped from him—before he could mount her.

With a growl, he pushed her thighs farther apart, making her breathing hitch. From fright or anticipation she couldn't say. She lay spread out before him, her hands roped to the jungle floor above her head, her thighs tied down to the ground making movement—and escape—impossible.

"Please!" she said louder, more pleadingly, her splintered brain making the connection between begging and the promise of release. Her head thrashed from side to side as the flower bud sucking on her clit grew more suctioning. "Oh God...I'm begging you!"

"Mmmm," he growled, his incisors bared. He palmed his massive cock and placed the tip at the opening to her pussy. "That's a good girl," he said in a patronizingly agreeable tone. "Such a sweet, biddable little wench..."

Her nostrils flared in renewed anger. Her jaw clenched as she narrowed her icy blue eyes at him.

Enraged at the insult, Zaab let out an ear-piercing bellow as he stared down at her, his acute green eyes narrowed in anger. She flinched when he pulled his cock away from her wet opening, then whimpered when he removed his hands from her breasts.

"I...I'm sorry!" she said truthfully, thrusting her hips up at him as best she could. "I won't do that again— I swear!" Anything—she'd do anything if only he'd fuck her, she thought hysterically.

The low growl in Zaab's throat told her the subtle rejoinder hadn't been quite forgotten by the arrogant male. And if her guess was accurate, he was still smarting from more than her show of defiance—he was still reeling from the knowledge that a human female had managed to elude him for more than six months.

Sometimes, mostly when sleeping alone in the stone caves late at night, she had often wondered if they had become the other's phantom obsession.

Dee ground her hips in a wanton, carnal gesture. Her breasts heaved up and down in time with her labored breathing. Beads of perspiration covered her torso. She no longer cared how pathetic she looked, no longer cared that the unthinkable had happened and she had been captured by her nemesis. Later, there would be time to think on that. For now, all she wanted was to be mounted.

"I swear I'll be good," she said throatily, her hips grinding up as she submissively lowered her eyelashes. "Please help me."

He was snarling down at her, the predator in him obvious, but she could also see his nostrils flexing, telling her he couldn't resist indulging in the scent of her arousal. She took comfort in that, hoping he would forget his anger long enough to put her out of the euphoric misery.

The flower bud at her clit began suctioning more vigorously, making her gasp. Her back arched, lifting up her breasts like two offerings. "Oh God." Her head fell back on the jungle floor, her nipples stabbing upwards. She hesitated for the briefest of moments, then turned her head, baring her neck to him.

The vines tightened their hold on her thighs, pinioning her motionless while the flower bud suckled juice from her cunt. She gritted her teeth, not wanting to come again, for her juice only made the bud suck harder and faster.

She was going to go mad. She was going to die of pleasure.

"Ah, you have bared your neck to me, lass," Zaab murmured in that arrogant tone of his. The baring of one's neck was a gesture of submission amongst predator peoples and they both knew it. Where her words had meant little, apparently her actions meant a lot.

His palms came down to knead her aching breasts again, making her moan. His fingers flicked at the nipples, inducing her back to arch and her hips to flare up. "Please," she whispered, tears clouding her vision. She was going to go insane—if he didn't help her she knew her mind would grow splintered. "I…I…"

His face engulfed her line of vision, blocking out the low-hanging moons overhead. All she could see was Zaab and his sharp green eyes. "You what?" he purred, knowing how difficult it was for her to plead with him. "A good wench always tells her Master what He needs to hear."

She swallowed against the lump in her throat, throwing her hips up at him again, wanting to grind her pussy against his cock. "I beg you," she said softly, quietly—pleadingly. "I beg you to fuck me."

His nostrils flared at the precise moment she heard the low growl in his throat resume. She wet her lips, praying that meant what she thought it did.

Zaab thrust her thighs apart again, his nostrils inhaling her scent. "I beg you to fuck me…what?" he growled.

"Master," she breathed out, her breasts heaving upward, wanting him to knead them a bit more roughly. "I beg you to fuck me, Master."

"And will you beg your Master to fuck you every night, slave?" he asked, the head of his thick cock again settling at the opening of her pussy.

"Yes."

"I didn't hear you, lass."

"Yes."

"And will you beg my brothers to fuck you as well, slave?"

Dee hesitated, not knowing what the correct answer was. She'd never gotten close enough to the Dementians to be aware of what transpired behind closed hut doors. She knew only of the things that transpired in public places. "Only if it pleases the Master," she hedged softly.

He purred again, telling her she'd answered well enough. "Good girl." He grabbed her breasts roughly, his dagger-like incisors bared. "And for the record, wench, you are not permitted to ever fuck another."

Until he sold her to someone else? Would he sell her to someone else?

Did it matter?

Zaab used his powerful legs to spread her already splayed thighs further apart. Grabbing the flower bud at the head, he popped it off her clit and snapped it in two. "Do you understand me, lass?"

"Yes."

"I didn't hear you, slave."

She wanted to cry. "Yes!" The euphoria was maddening, horrific...

With a primitive growl, he thrust his huge cock inside her enveloping flesh, impaling her cunt in one deep thrust. She could hear the suctioning sound her pussy made as he slowly pulled back and stroked out of her, as if her body was trying to pull his cock back in to the hilt.

"Oh God," she moaned, trying in vain to throw her hips at him the way she wanted to. She could see his teeth gritting, the vein at his neck bulging. She wanted him to thrust fast and deep inside her. "Oh God — please."

Zaab gave her what she wanted, growling low in his throat as he plunged in and out of her cunt over and over, again and again. He rode her hard, like an animal, impaling her enveloping flesh like a battering ram.

His flowing black mane of hair tickled her breasts, running like silk over her nipples as he fucked her. "Do you like this, slave?" he arrogantly ground out, the muscles in his arms bulging as he repeatedly buried his thick cock deep inside her.

Dee's head thrashed from side to side, sexual euphoria overwhelming her. "Yes."

"Yes what?"

"Yes, Master."

He rewarded her obedient answer with harder, deeper strokes, threading her golden hair around one hand as his other hand kneaded her breasts and played with her nipples. He rode her body ruthlessly, going primal on her cunt, marking her flesh with his scent.

She closed her eyes on a moan, her hands tied above her head, her breasts jiggling, as the Alpha Male of the Mantus Hoard fucked her long and hard. She came over and over, again and again, moaning and groaning, marking him with her scent as much as he meant to mark her with his.

"Beg for my cum, slave," Zaab growled, his cock plunging into her flesh in fast strokes. "Beg your Master to mark you."

"Yes — please — Master…"

Dee's half-delirious gaze clashed with his alert green one. She could see his jaw clenching, his nostrils flaring. Perversely, the knowledge that she was the cause of such a rigid, controlled male showing even that much emotion made her impossibly wetter.

Zaab lowered his face to her neck as he continued to mount her, a warning growl hissing low in his throat. She tensed, realizing as she did that he was displaying his dominance over her. He could slice through her jugular at any time, that growl resonating through her eardrum said. He could kill her, he could fuck her, he could enslave her…

Dee gasped when his incisors scraped against her jugular vein, fear causing her eyes to close tightly. He grunted, as if pleased she had at last realized who it was that held all power over her.

"Relax, lass," he purred near her ear as he stroked in and out of her cunt. "If you're a biddable little wench," he ground out, his thrusts coming faster and harder as he wrapped his hand more securely around her hair, "you will know my pleasure instead of my wrath."

He took her hard then — harder than ever before. His hips pistoned back and forth as he plunged his cock in and out of her suctioning flesh, his jaw clenched tightly as he drove them both toward orgasm.

"Yes," Dee groaned, unable to move, unable to do anything but lie there and feel him fucking her. "Oh God."

She came violently — convulsively, her loud moan echoing throughout the highlander alien jungle. "Yes — oh God yes." Her thighs shook like leaves in a storm as her head thrashed madly from side to side. She groaned when his thrusts became impossibly faster, more primal and animalistic.

"Who owns this cunt?" Zaab ground out, the fingers threaded through her hair clenching the strands tighter. "Tell me."

"Master!" Dee cried out, another violent orgasm crashing over her. "Master Zaab!"

He growled low in his throat as he stiffened above her, thrusting in and out of her pussy like an animal — like a predator. She opened her eyes to the sight of his clenched jaw, his gritted teeth, his corded muscles, his bared incisors...

Zaab threw his head back on a deafening roar that bubbled up from his throat and reverberated throughout the jungle. He impaled her cunt over and over, never stopping his thrusting, as he pumped her cunt full of cum. She cried out at the sound, her eyes widening, the instinctive need to clasp her hands over her ears thwarted by the vines that held her pinioned to the cold ground of the jungle.

"Mine," he hissed into her ear as his climax began to wane. "My cunt."

He continued to stroke his massive erection in and out of her flesh, his cock still not satiated. But then neither was her body replete. The hallucinogen had made it so it would be hours, perhaps days, before her pussy felt satisfied.

The general fucked her for endless hours that night, stopping occasionally to feed and care for her. And he did take good care of her, Dee would later admit. He forced her to drink liquids even when she didn't feel thirsty, growled at her to eat the food bits he placed in her mouth even when she complained she wasn't hungry.

And always he fucked her. Violently. Endlessly. Gluttonously.

After hours and hours of mating, he finally cut the vines from her body, freeing her. But he didn't let her go, of course—didn't give her the chance to escape from him again. He twined his large, warm body around her smaller one instead, providing her with warmth as they drifted off into slumber.

Chapter Three

ಐ

Zaab carried his naked slave on his back as they made their way through the highlander jungle. Harnessed to him by a leather-like contraption Dementians often used when carrying their young, he was taking no chances with either his captive's safety or with the chance that she might escape him for a third time.

Dee Ellison—he knew her birth name. It had been the first piece of information he had extracted from the slave Zidia when she had been captured by the Mantus Hoard and sold to the Myng Hoard.

Zidia had tried to escape Dementia with Dee, he knew, but of course the lasses had failed. On a planet where no female births ever occurred it would be foolhardy to let even one wench of childbearing years leave it. Without the humanoid female slaves available to breed, there would be no such thing as Dementia, for their numbers would die out until their species was extinct—a fact Dementian males were careful to keep quiet about to outsiders.

His warlord friend Jek Q'an Ri had once told him that mayhap his species should try love on the wenches instead of slavery. But Zaab failed to see the difference between the wife of a warrior and the zahbi of a Dementian. Neither was given the choice concerning whether or not they could leave the male who had captured them. Neither was permitted to touch another male after mating.

Insofar as Zaab was concerned, Dee Ellison's fate had been sealed from their first meeting—and her first escape.

The first time the general had laid eyes on her she had been attempting to steal a spacecraft vessel from Stone City with the slave Zidia. His fighters had captured Zidia within minutes, but Dee Ellison had managed to escape into the lowlander jungle.

If he hadn't been immediately taken with the lass upon first glance, then by the time the wench had managed to thwart his attempts at capturing her, he had been consumed with her. Zaab had thought back on the lass often after that eve, wondering if she had met a bad end, wondering too if she'd been captured by another male.

Three months later Zaab had caught Dee stealing meat from the communal hut of the Mantus Hoard. His first reaction had been surprise at seeing her—alive and not yet enslaved to another. His second reaction had been admiration, for 'twould have taken more than a wee bit of cunning to survive alone and unaided within the jungle for so long. His third reaction had been a mix of lust and possessiveness—he wanted her and he wanted no other male to touch her. His fourth reaction had been anger, for the wench had managed—again—to escape him.

The admiration, lust, possessiveness, and anger coalesced into obsession. He was obsessed with Dee Ellison, he knew. Mayhap he would always be obsessed with her.

"I'm thirsty," she whispered from the harness strapped to his back, the first words she had spoken in hours. "May I have a drink?" When he didn't answer right away, she amended her statement. "May I have a drink, Master?"

Her voice was scratchy, her throat parched. He hated that he cared so much, but there it was. Ammunition she could use against him if she knew of his obsession. He steeled his jaw and answered her. "We will stop at the next stream, slave."

Fifteen minutes later, Zaab's green eyes watched as his naked obsession drank from the pure waters of a highlander stream. She was on her hands and knees, her back to him, cupping water and lifting it to her face for refreshment. His gaze strayed to her cunt.

Puffy. Pink. Pretty.

His.

Dee gasped when Zaab's hands roughly grabbed her hips, then groaned when he slid his huge cock into her pussy from behind. "Beg me, slave," she heard him grit out. "Beg me."

On her hands and knees, impaled to the hilt, her sensitive breasts dangling, she had never been more aroused. Or more worried about her body's reaction to the general.

He slowly slid his cock out, then back in, teasing her with the promise of ecstasy. She shuddered, wanting more. "I beg you," she murmured.

"I didn't hear you, lass." He gave her two more long, deep strokes.

"I beg you!" she gasped. "Please fuck my pussy, Master."

He palmed her breasts from behind. "Whose pussy?" he growled.

"My—your—your pussy." She groaned when his fingers began plucking at her nipples. "Please fuck your pussy, Master!"

He took her hard, animalistically, plunging in and out of her flesh like the predator he was. His growls punctured the night, his masculine scent perfumed the air.

"Harder," Dee moaned, throwing her hips back at him. "More."

His growls grew louder, more reverberating, as he fucked her harder, the sound of their flesh meeting aphrodisiac. "Do you like this, little lass?" he ground out. His fingers dug into the padding of her hips as he pummeled her cunt with deep, possessive strokes.

"I love it," she gasped. It was the truth. An unsettling truth. She would be no man's slave.

Dee came violently, her entire body shuddering on a groan loud enough to wake the dead. She could feel Zaab's cock ruthlessly plunging into her from behind, over and over, again and again. She could hear his low, possessive growl, could feel his powerful muscles tensing...

"Zahbi," he growled as she felt his hot cum pour into her. "Mine."

Panting for air, her eyes closed in a euphoria more hedonistic than the one brought on by the vines. She was on the verge of orgasming again when she cried out instead, shocked and in pain when two incisors sliced into her shoulder. "Zaab—don't kill me! No—please!"

"Mine," he growled against her shoulder as he lapped up the blood the pinpricks had made. "All mine."

Dee came harder than she'd ever come before, moaning and groaning while she met each of his animalistic thrusts with one of her own. The orgasm was endless, intense—all-consuming. Blood rushed to her face, heating it. Blood rushed to her nipples, elongating them until they stabbed Zaab's palms.

"Oh God," she whimpered as they came down from the high together, "oh God."

Chapter Four
One week later

જી

Dee didn't know what to make of anything. She was Zaab's slave—one slave in a harem of thirty. And yet the only woman he touched, the only woman he even looked at, was her. The other females were but serving girls to him, whereas she was...well she didn't know what she was. She only knew that she hadn't been given much in the way of chores beyond feeding him, bathing him and fucking him.

Confusing.

Equally confusing was the fact that she was growing to care for him. She didn't know how that had come to happen, or when precisely he had gotten under her skin, only that he had.

Zaab was rough and stern—but only to others. He was ferocious and deadly—but only to others. Where Dee was concerned, Zaab was different somehow. His speech was gentler when she was around. His conduct was more relaxed and personable with her than with anyone else. Almost as if...

She snorted at her thoughts. Dementian males did not love. Emotions like that were not in their genetic makeup.

Were they?

She sighed. Did it matter?

Naked—for slaves were always naked—Dee padded over to the window of the large thatch and stone hut that was Zaab's home and stared out of it, her thoughts a million miles away. She'd been in Dementia for over a year now and was a much different woman from the carefree one who'd once called Earth home.

Would Earth feel like home now, she wondered. Would she be able to forget this past year and fit in with other humans again if she found a way to return? Did she want to?

One thing was for certain, Dee thought on a sigh. It would be difficult, to say the least, to pretend that she was just like every other human. She would be forced to keep her silence about Dementia for fear of being institutionalized. She would be forced to do her damnedest to erase the past from her memories for fear that she'd slip up and start talking about life in the alien jungle.

And she would be forced to find pleasure with a human male. As if a human male could ever hope to compare…

"What troubles you, lass?" Zaab asked the question before leaning down to place a kiss on her shoulder.

Dee jumped, startled, for she hadn't heard him come in. "You frightened me," she breathed out, turning around to face him.

He snorted at that. "'Tis doubtful that ten charging liats could frighten you." He lowered his face to her chest, popped a nipple into his mouth and began suckling.

She smiled, proud that he found her a force to be reckoned with. And then she moaned, turned on by the attention he was lavishing on her breasts.

Zaab raised his head a few minutes later, his green eyes clashing with her blue ones. He reached for her golden hair, his fingers running through it. "'Tis beautiful, lass. As are you."

More soft words. At this rate, she'd never want to leave him. "Thank you," she whispered.

They stood there in silence, gazing at each other, neither of them speaking a word. But finally, long moments later, Zaab broke the silence. "Come to my bed, zahbi," he said softly, "I cannot sleep without you in it."

Don't do this, she thought. *Don't make me love you.*

But when he laced his fingers through hers and gently guided her to the bed, she knew deep inside that it was too late.

She had been lost to Earth from the moment their gazes first clashed in Stone City.

Chapter Five
One week later
The Feast of Beginnings

ဆာ

General Zaab, the Alpha Male of the Mantus Hoard, the Supreme Master of the Highlanders, leaned back in his chair as he watched three naked slave girls dance for him. This eve was special for the feast they were partaking of was held in honor of Jaaker, the male ape-god who had breathed life into the first of their species.

Zaab cared not that the males of his hoard were touching and fondling the three slaves as they danced by. Slaves were expected to give their bodies not only to the master, but to his friends and family members as well. Or more to the point, they were expected to give their bodies freely for the use of any Dementian male, until she was claimed as a zahbi by the male who impregnated her.

In the eyes of Zaab, Dee was already his wife. Yet he knew the others would not see it thusly. Her belly was not ripe with child, therefore 'twas impossible to make a public claim on her. He had marked her privately when he'd bitten into her shoulder that eve at the stream, yet insofar as he knew none of the Dementian males had seen her branding.

He knew they hadn't. He'd permitted no other males to be near her.

Zaab's green eyes darted up when he saw Dee walk into the communal hut carrying trenchers. His entire body stilled. Who had told Dee to come to the feast? Had he not given orders that—

"Such beautiful breasts you have, my dear," the leader of the Myng Hoard told Dee as he cupped them, pulling her to his side. "You have nipples like berries."

Dee blushed, clearly not knowing what to do or say.

"Bend over, wench," another gorilla fighter called out. "I want to see what your cunt looks like. Mayhap 'tis worthy of milking my cock."

Zaab exploded from his chair, leaping onto the table before them in one swift action. Growling, he backhanded the fighter who had thought to fuck her, blood spurting from the male's nose as he fell to the ground.

Dee turned wide blue eyes on him.

"What is this?" the leader of the Myng Hoard asked, offended. "You have insulted my fighter!"

"He has insulted me!" Zaab bellowed. "That wench he thought to fuck is my zahbi!"

Dee's mouth dropped open. It was then that Zaab realized she'd had no idea what zahbi meant...until this moment.

"Well I...I...did not know," the leader sputtered. "You have not publicly claimed her, General Zaab. She wears no belly chain." The leader of the Myng Hoard, clearly not wanting bad blood with the Mantus Hoard, nodded respectfully down to Dee. "Congratulations on your pregnancy, lass. 'Tis honored you are to bear the heir of the Mantus."

Zaab glanced away, preparing to be publicly humiliated. The moment Dee told them the truth he would look the fool for caring so deeply for a wench he had not—

"Thank you," Dee said simply.

Zaab's body stilled.

"I'm sorry you were confused, but he was planning to publicly claim me at the feast tonight."

Zaab glanced up at her, warily meeting her gaze.

"Weren't you, Zaab?"

"Err…" He was shocked. He could scarcely believe Dee had defended him and his honor before the others. "Aye," he muttered.

"Well then," the leader of the Myng Hoard interrupted, his attempt to keep any potential brawls at bay obvious. "Let us get on with the claiming then."

* * * * *

A little embarrassed, but mostly aroused, Dee sat on Zaab's lap, her back to his chest, and eased her pussy down onto his cock until she enveloped him. She heard his grunt of pleasure when he was seated to the hilt, then moaned when his fingers began plucking at her nipples.

The gorilla fighters watched, her legs splayed wide before them, as she began to bounce up and down on Zaab's cock, moaning and groaning from the pleasure of it. She knew they could hear the suctioning sound her cunt made as it enveloped him, knew they could smell her arousal as her tits jiggled up and down for their viewing pleasure.

But then that was the point. For Zaab to publicly bring her pleasure, for Zaab to publicly brand her as his own.

"Beg me," Zaab murmured in her ear. "Beg your Master for his cum, slave."

"Please," Dee gasped, bouncing up and down as hard and as fast as she could on his thick cock. "Please cum in your cunt, Master!"

She groaned when Zaab grabbed her roughly by the hips and, with a growl, began pumping his cock into her pussy like an animal. She closed her eyes, her head falling back on his chest, and bared her neck to him in front of one and all while he fucked her.

His hand reached around and he began stroking her clit while he lowered his face to her neck. She came the moment his incisors broke the skin there, moaning loudly as she rode out the climax.

This time he had marked her neck, not her shoulder. She wasn't precisely certain of the deeper meaning, but she was certain there was one.

The gorilla fighters applauded, shouting out bawdy remarks. "Fuck her harder!" one bellowed. "Spread the lass's cunt lips apart for us!" another shouted.

Zaab, arrogant as ever, did both. Dee closed her eyes and reveled in another orgasm, gluttonously loving every moment of it. She'd never been showcased like this before, had never been fucked in front of hundreds of men while they all sat around and watched her moan and groan with pleasure.

When it was over, when Zaab spurted his hot cum into her cunt on a roar, a belly chain was handed to her Master, which was then placed around her middle.

Dee glanced over her shoulder and smiled up at him. Their bodies were still joined together. "I guess this means I'm your wife now."

Zaab leaned down and kissed the tip of her nose. "Aye. Your Master will always cherish you, little lass."

Epilogue

Naked, Dee rubbed her belly, which was ripe with Zaab's heir. She lay down on the sweet, fragrant grass, then spread her legs wide open for her Master. She smiled when he lowered his face to her cunt and began to lazily lap at it. "Mmm. That feels so good, Zaab."

He purred low in his throat as he playfully nibbled on her clit. "Mmm. It tastes so good, zahbi."

She closed her eyes and smiled dreamily while he pleasured her outside under the warm rays of the red-tinted sky. Long minutes later, when they'd both had their fill, she made an announcement that would sound ludicrous coming from any woman but Dee. "We're going to have a girl."

Zaab's body stilled. He raised his face from between her legs. "'Tis sorry I am, Cherished One," he said quietly as he gently rubbed her belly. "But Dementians can only breed males."

"We're having a daughter," Dee said simply, nodding firmly.

Zaab snorted, a half grin on his face. "I suppose were it possible you would find the means to bear one."

She chuckled at that. "Yep." And then she reached out a hand. "Come up here and lie beside me where I can see you over my belly, you lovable oaf."

"Oaf," he growled, coming up to lie beside her. "Is that any way for a zahbi to talk to the Master who loves her?"

She smiled, snuggling into his warmth and resting her head on his muscled chest.

Together they fell asleep under the warmth of the red-tinted sky.

NEVER A SLAVE
�‍

Chapter One

The jungle outside Valor City
6049 Y.Y. (Yessat Years)

Jesus Christ — what a bloody week!

It was bad enough that he was the only paying customer at The Smiling Faces and Peaceful Hearts retreat who had managed to flunk out, having failed to find his wretched peace. It was bad enough to learn upon his return to England that Letty, his wife of five years, had decided she was a lesbian and left him for a barmaid who was nicknamed "The Tongue". It was worse still to discover that Letty'd not only taken his pride with her, but his dog Max as well. Of the two, he'd have picked Max as a companion any day of the week — at least the dog was loyal.

But this…

Lord Julian Jameson scowled at nothing in particular as he dashed through the maroon jungle of…wherever in the hell he was. His sweat-slicked muscles bulging, his bronzed, naked torso glistening, he decided that nothing, but nothing could be worse than *this*.

He had no notion as to where he was and even less of a clue as to how he'd gotten here. He was fairly certain he was not — unfathomable as it sounded — still on Earth. If the five moons hovering atop the skyline hadn't given that fact away, then the technologically advanced weaponry he'd seen the females here sporting would have.

For seven solid days and nights Julian had been on the run from women. Women he was fairly certain wanted to make him into some manner of sex slave. As incredulous as it sounded even to himself—namely that any female should want to engage in intercourse with him at all let alone make sex-giving his sole purpose in life—it had taken but an hour's worth of eavesdropping in the last tiny village he'd holed up in to ascertain that, indeed, sex and servitude appeared to be all that men were good for around this place. The irony, of course, was not lost on him.

Julian's sex life up until this point could best be described as nonexistent. He was a handsome man with his golden good looks and tall, muscular physique, he supposed. Blond hair and brown eyes, dimples that defined his cheeks on the rare occasions he smiled—he'd been described more than once as a visual study in contrasts. Such mattered very little when you were wed to a woman who wanted nothing to do with you.

Once upon a time, he had thought that Letty would make the perfect wife. She was beautiful, learned and had pretended to be head over heels in love with him. He had wasted no time in setting his sights on marrying her, deciding she would make not only an ideal viscountess his parents could approve of, but an ideal lover as well. Julian had, he now realized, been mistaken on all accounts.

He had courted Letty for over a year before they'd married. During that year he had wanted so very much to bed her, to know what it felt like to sink into her exquisite flesh and pump away like a mad jackrabbit. He had thought Letty wanted the same thing. But as "The Tongue" could surely attest, that was never the case.

Having been raised by extremely conservative and devoutly religious parents who'd forced him into attending boys' schools his entire life, Julian had been a virgin on his wedding night. Waiting had been more difficult than words could express, for he thought about sex day and night. But, conversely, he had shared his parents' religious views back then and had wanted to wait because he felt it was the morally proper thing to do. And so he'd waited for Letty, taking solace in the knowledge that once he married her he would be given free reign to go wild on her body, to make love to his wife at whim.

That, unfortunately, was not to be.

Julian knew that people often wondered why it is that he never smiled. But then those very people weren't aware of the fact that, a wedding ceremony and five years worth of marriage later, Lord Julian Jameson was still a virgin. A thirty-year-old, hornier-than-all-bloody-hell virgin who, as idiotic as it sounded, remained faithful to a wife who refused his touch.

He frowned, wondering for the first time in seven days if he should just end the wretched chase, let himself get caught by the huntresses and be done with it all—his virginity included. But then, engaging in a bout of sex and suffering the indignity of sexual slavery were two entirely different things.

And so here he was, dashing as fast as his bare feet could carry him, doing his damnedest to avoid being captured like some manner of undignified prey. The soles of his feet were callused, his feet scratched up and a bit bloody from running, but it didn't matter. He had no intention of stopping—not now or ever—for he had no notion as to what these huntresses wanted with him. Sex, or so he assumed, but beyond that…

Julian had tried his hand at eavesdropping on the females who were hunting him the last time they had stopped and made camp. Thinking to find out why precisely it was that they wanted to capture him to begin with, he had realized inside of five seconds that no answers would be soon in coming.

Unfortunately, Julian thought as he made a sharp left turn and ran toward a dense patch of maroon shrubbery to use as camouflage, they didn't speak any of the three languages he'd been schooled in. But then he didn't need to understand what the women were saying to comprehend the fact that these particular females were pack-hunters. Pack-hunters who hunted men.

"My'at fena, mala ra!" a female voice called out.

The sound chilled him as it reached his ears, the shout sounding almost victorious. Which could only mean that…

Oh no.

Julian grunted as a strong pulse of energy hit him full force in the back. He bellowed as he stumbled to the ground and rolled, maroon mud staining his chest and face a dark red as he tumbled down the side of a hillock.

Damn! He needed to get up and run, but he had been rendered immobile by whatever it was that had hit him. *I've got to get out of here…*

It was the last thought he was to entertain as a free man.

Julian bellowed a final cry of anger before landing face-first in a black puddle. The cold feel of a handcuff-like mechanism was clasped unforgivingly around either wrist as he lay there in the sludge unable to move, a strange fatigue overwhelming him.

It was over, he knew, his heart rate thumping like a rock in his chest courtesy of whatever type of energy beam they'd managed to fell him with. His body automatically tensed up as he felt the hand of a huntress glide over his muscled buttocks.

Julian closed his eyes, giving in to the fatigue, realizing that escape would have to be put on hold until he woke up.

Chapter Two

ဢ

He slowly awoke to the feel of several female hands touching him intimately. On his chest, on his abs, on his cock…

Shit, Julian thought as his stomach muscles clenched and he expelled a breath of air on a hiss. Someone was even cupping his tight balls and massaging them.

He fought within himself, his traitorous body loving the long-denied sensations being evoked by exploratory female hands whilst his mind abhorred the idea that he should want this. He halfheartedly tried to break away from their touches, only to realize he was, although standing upright, chained against a soft but unyielding disk-like structure. It rotated occasionally, making him aware of its roundness. He tried to open his eyes, but a blindfold prevented him from doing so.

"'Tis a wicked big cock this creature possesses," boomed an authoritative female voice. "Feel free to inspect it before the auction begins, but no fucking it. The right to deflower the innocent creature belongs to whichever of you will leave here his Mistress."

Julian's nostrils flared at the rather delicate description. His anger was so acute that he'd almost neglected to notice that he was somehow able to understand what was being said about him. He would have thought more on the subject, but another female voice broke his train of thought.

"Aye, 'tis true," she said breathlessly. "His manpart is nigh unto as big as the rest of him."

Julian's jaw clenched. Against his volition, said manpart swelled even further. And then further still when his body's reaction met with a bunch of ooing and ahhing from his enraptured audience.

He gritted his teeth. Bloody hell. This was just too much. If it wasn't for the fact he was fairly confident he was headed for a life in chains, this scenario would have been like some depraved fantasy come true. The sort he'd entertained whilst having sex for one all these lonely years.

A small, wet mouth began to nibble on the head of his cock. He sucked in his breath, for some reason not having expected that. The mouth toyed with him a bit before it opened up wide, inviting him all the way in to the back of her talented throat.

A second mouth latched onto one of his balls, forcing a stifled moan from him. The mouth played with him in such a way that brought to mind bobbing for apples. A third mouth latched onto his other testicle, sucking it like candy whilst the first mouth greedily suckled his rigid shaft. A fourth and fifth mouth found either of his nipples.

He groaned, unable to suppress the sound.

"The creature responds well to stimulation," a spectator mused. "Mayhap I shall taste his man juice after Her Worthiness drinks of it. If she finishes before the auction."

"His scent is very virginal," a second woman murmured. "Mmm. I so want his cock for mine own."

"'Tis a healthy man sac he possesses," another voice chimed in. "Leastways, 'tis a certainty his cock can make plenty of juice for all of us."

Julian's penis swelled impossibly further. It was almost too much to believe that any woman should want to do this to him, let alone all of these women. His only experience with a female, however, had been with a wife who refused to have anything to do with him.

He shouldn't want this, his mind screamed, but his body refused to listen. His cock was being pleasured for the first time in his life by someone other than himself. And greedily at that. And his balls, and his nipples…

Bloody, bloody, *bloody* hell.

The mouth working his shaft slowed. He expelled a breath of air, not wanting to admit he wished she'd go faster.

The talented mouth took her time, furthering her intimate knowledge of him with heady, leisurely sucks. This went on for what felt like hours—too slow for release, too damn good to ignore. Before long he was unconsciously trying to buck his tethered hips toward the mouth, his body aching to be finished off.

Julian groaned when the talented mouth working up and down his shaft took him in so far he swore he could feel her tonsils. He gritted his teeth when she picked up the pace. He could imagine in his mind's eye the image of her face bobbing feverishly back and forth whilst she sucked on his cock.

I'm coming, he thought, unable to suppress it even though his mind didn't want to give his captors what it was they were wishing to extract from him. *Oh – God –*

The mouth sucked him frenziedly, making him moan loud and long. The other mouths worked him just as greedily, but it was the woman commanding his shaft that held him spellbound.

"He's going to spurt," a spectator mused.

"Aye. And greedy Klykka will drain his nectar dry."

Julian groaned, his body tensing up as it prepared to climax. Perspiration dotted his brow. His heart rate was over the top. The mouth worked faster, and although he was blindfolded, he could still sense from the brisk movements bodily jarring him that her head was bobbing up and down.

"Oh shit," he breathed out in a language the women couldn't understand. "Oh *God*."

He came loud and hard, his entire body convulsing as his cock spurted what felt to be an endless stream of seed into the awaiting, hungry mouth. He gritted his teeth when he heard her make an appreciative *mmm* sound as she drank of him, then groaned when she sucked briskly from the tiny hole in his cock's head to make sure she hadn't missed a single drop.

"'Tis time for the auction," an authoritative voice boomed out. He scarcely heard it, his mind and body reeling. "Klykka, you must step away from the creature anon. Bid upon him if you so desire."

"I want my turn," he heard another female voice call out. "You can't expect me to bid upon a creature I don't know the taste of!"

Depraved fantasies, he thought, half delirious. His lips pinched together as he glowered. Perhaps he'd gone mad during his last masturbation session and his mind was making this all up.

"There is no more time," the auctioneer said in an unbending tone. "The auction must begin anon. You can see for yourself how big and brawny he is. I have testified as to his cunning and thinking abilities. He would breed worthy daughters for any High Mystik."

Julian stilled as he came down from the realm of climax and crash-landed into the realm of reality. He was wanted as…*a breeder*? Like a bloody *horse*?

His nostrils flared. An action that didn't go unnoticed by the woman named Klykka who had been suckling his shaft. Her soft laughter reached his ears.

"Fear not, lusty one," a dark, smoky voice said into the whorl of his ear. He found himself wondering what she looked like, then discarded the question altogether. It hardly mattered. He would run at first opportunity no matter what she looked like. "You will come to love me. 'Tis a vow I give unto you."

And then she was walking away, leaving him blindfolded and tethered to the strange disk-like structure that held him captive and suspended from the ground. He sighed as the disk began to move, wondering how in the hell he had gotten into this mess and, more importantly, how in the hell he would get out of it.

Depraved fantasies, he supposed, were best left to one's imagination.

Chapter Three

ဢ

Klykka Gy'at Li, High Mystik to the sector that bore her surname, watched through shrewd violet eyes as seven creatures were transported to the center stage within the black crystal coliseum. She had trekked to Valor City with the intention of buying a slave or two to add to her harem, having grown bored as of late with the males she already owned.

She had never thought in her wildest dreams that she would end up attending a breeder auction instead of a slave auction—mating with a male was something she had never before considered. But this humanoid man…

She had known the minute she'd spotted him, his sleeping body being loaded onto a *kazza* disk, that the pack-hunters would not be sending this prime specimen to the slave block. He was too fine of form, face and cock—too perfect in his maleness. When legends of his prowess, namely the fact that he had outwitted a team of talented pack-hunters for seven days, reached her ears, Klykka knew for a certainty that such a cunning male was mating material. He would go for a high sum on the breeding block—not a lower sum like the slaves commanded.

She could scarce believe she was standing here, bidding against other High Mystiks for the right to own one of the seven males hoisted up onto the platform, and yet here she was. Wenches of lesser rank than hers would probably bid on him too, though 'twas doubtful any less than a High Mystik possessed the credits it would take to barter for him.

That was just fine by her, she thought through narrowed eyes as the High Mystik of the Quanti sector placed a bid on a male Klykka held no interest in. It helped to eliminate some of the competition.

Klykka's gaze strayed back toward the creature—*her* creature. Leastways, she would own him this moon-rising without a doubt. None present could afford to outbid her. 'Twas now just a question of how many credits she'd be set back before the male belonged to her.

A strange sense of impending fate had swamped her senses the very first time she'd laid eyes on him. Prior to the actual auction, during the time when potential bidders were permitted to freely inspect the chattel, she had wanted none but herself to drink of his essence. An odd feeling, that. Especially for a wench possessing a large harem who was long accustomed to sharing her chattel with others. But this chattel…

Was hers.

She didn't wish to share him. Ever. Not even with her beloved sisters. He had a commanding presence about him even whilst in chains…so different from the weak-willed freemen of Galis who were prone toward excessive emotion and trying to get their way with their mates through tears and sexual manipulation.

"The next creature up for bid is this six-and-a-quarter-footer," the auctioneer boomed out, gaining Klykka's undivided attention. She watched as her future mate's cock was pumped back and forth, swelling it mightily until it rested long and thick against his navel.

He groaned, causing her to frown. She disliked watching him being wench-handled by others.

"See you for yourselves the pleasure this chattel can give unto you. But this creature, fair wenches, is possessed of more than a wicked big manpart. He is also possessed of superior cunning and intellect..."

Klykka took a deep breath and blew it out, listening as Gar'az listed all the chattel's attributes. Quick. Strong. Cunning. Physically well-honed. Feisty. Virginal. In a few words, a perfect breeder. Any daughters he put in Klykka's belly would be strong and keen warrior women.

His blindfold was removed a moment later, revealing his handsome visage up close and awake for the first time. She bit her lip, her hearts rate thumping pleasurably in her chest.

Her nipples hardened just looking upon him. She could scarcely wait to claim him. She knew that the auctioneer wasn't lying and that he was indeed a virgin, for she hadn't smelled the scent of another female upon him whilst she'd drunk of his essence. Only she would couple with him—only her.

"These are rare attributes amongst males of any species, so he won't be sold for cheap. Come now! Do I hear an opening bid of ten thousand credits?"

Klykka raised her arm high and held up a fist—the means of declaring oneself in auctions on Galis. "I bid unto you ten thousand, Mistress."

"Do I hear ten thousand and five?"

"Ten thousand and five, Mistress!" the High Mystik from Lo'am shouted out.

Klykka frowned. As if a wench from Lo'am, High Mystik or no, could afford to outbid her. "Eleven."

"Twelve."

"Thirteen."

This went on until the sum reached into the twenties, whereupon the competition folded, just as Klykka had known it would. She smiled a predator's satisfaction at a prey well and truly caught, her gaze locking with the male whom she now owned.

He was curious about her and about his fate — she could see it in his dark eyes. But there was more emotion there than mere curiosity.

He was angry, she could tell. Angry and feisty. Mayhap he even thought he could find a way to escape her. That would, of course, never happen.

"Your Worthiness," the auctioneer called out to Klykka, "your creature awaits you. Pay for him and he shall be released unto you."

Lust knotted Klykka's belly. Her gaze strayed to her new mate.

One dark, imperious eyebrow rose in response to the chattel who dared look upon his Mistress in ire. Oh aye, he was angry. Well and truly feisty.

A small smile tugged at the corners of her lips. Good.

'Twas turning out to be the most interesting moon-rising of her forty-one Yessat Years.

* * * * *

Julian's eyes narrowed at the two warrior women who were escorting him from the platform. He was completely naked, wearing nothing but a slave's torque and chains. The warriors paid his anger no heed whatsoever, their attention instead focused on keeping him manacled. The female who had purchased him apparently thought herself above the arduous task of restraining him, for she was walking several feet ahead of the group, her body language arrogant and self-assured.

She was a woman used to commanding others. A woman long accustomed to having her every wish granted.

A woman who would soon rue the day she had enslaved him.

Upon purchasing him, Julian's captor had boldly strutted up to where he was hoisted above the swell of the crowd, placed some bizarre-looking device that made a whirring sound on his penis, detonated it then walked away with nary a word. She'd paid him no further attention, leaving him to hiss in pain as the warriors who now stood at either side of him cut him down from the harness.

He had paid attention during the auction and so realized that his captor's name was Klykka. She was a beautiful woman, he loathed to admit. Stunning, in fact. He had no trouble ascertaining as much, for the dress of the women in this world was all but non-existent. Shimmering G-strings of assorted colors, sandals with straps that criss-crossed all the way up to the knee—and that was it. Otherwise their bodies were bared, their breasts and derrières exposed for all to see.

He smiled grimly. Depraved fantasies indeed.

The body of his captor was long and athletic, her skin colored a sleek bronze with a hint of gold. The brief glimpse he'd gotten of her from the front had revealed an exotically pretty face with luminescent violet eyes that glowed just a bit, framed by a mane of dark hair that swept down to just above her buttocks in a cascade of ebony ringlets. Her breasts were full and large, the perky pink nipples a sharp contrast against bronze skin.

Her backside, unfortunately, was just as provocative as the front. Her buttocks were athletically sculpted, yet still plush and round with soft feminine curves. A dimple above either buttock accented them, drawing his gaze again and again.

Julian frowned. He was growing erect just looking at her and he hated himself for it. He would do well to remember that this woman thought to enslave him.

The warrior women who held his chains came to a halt, forcing him to stop as well. He watched Klykka disappear into a tent-like structure, the odd material constructed from what looked to be silk scarves of a color he had no word for in English.

The warrior to his left spoke. "We enter the portal that will take us to the Gy'at Li sector, unworthy one." He raised an eyebrow at the name she'd called him by, but as usual his reaction was given no attention. "You are to do what you are told, when you are told and how you are told. If you are defiant, I will take great joy in whipping you, aye?"

His nostrils flared. "Let me go," he hissed.

"If you've half a brain," the second warrior instructed, "you will seek to pleasure Her Worthiness in all things." She smiled at him, her kindness surprising after the insulting way in which the first warrior had spoken to him. "'Tis an honor you have been granted, serving our Lady and her cunt in all things. Remember that and act accordingly lest you be sent to the gulch pits of Tryston for treason against your Mistress."

Julian frowned. Beyond the word cunt, he had no idea what most of what she'd just said meant, but he wisely held his tongue. If he could get the warrior on his right alone later, he would put questions to her. For now, his instincts told him, he would do well to remain silent in front of the warrior to his left.

Julian said nothing as he was led into the portal. He glanced around curiously as they entered the silk tent, surprised to find that there was nothing inside it. One moment the landscape had been a flat, placid purple and a blink later they were spit out onto mountainous obsidian terrain.

A vast village constructed of shimmering white crystal curled around the base of a gigantic black mountain. The layout was vast—as big as any modern English city. He couldn't help but to stare a bit wide-eyed, for he'd never seen a sight quite so spectacular. Or peculiar.

From the position where they stood far above the city centre, he could make out that the people of this place moved about not by planes, trains and automobiles, but by large birds. He forgot himself for a moment, forgot too that he had been brought here as a slave, and allowed himself to stare like an open-mouthed simpleton.

He had to be dreaming. Those birds brought to mind old science fiction novels he'd read as a young lad.

A large, winged creature transporting three riders loomed near, giving him his first close-up view. The nearer the beast drew to where he stood, the easier it was to see that what had looked like a bird from a distance was physically more like a winged monkey in its appearance.

Brilliant. He'd gone from science fiction to Oz in the matter of a few moments. He shook his head and sighed as he glanced away. Nothing made sense here.

A huge palace constructed of what looked to be purple crystal sat atop the peak of the tallest black mountain on the horizon. He focused his attention on it. And where it sat in relation to the portal they'd just passed through. It didn't take a genius to figure out, after all, that the palace belonged to Klykka—and that this was where he would be taken.

"Come, foul creature," the warrior to his left spat as she tugged at the chain fastened to the torque about his neck. He grunted, the look he threw her in reaction letting her know that her loathing of him was mutual. She ignored it. "We will take the tunnels to the harem chamber and then, thank the goddess, my duty with you is done."

Harem chamber, Julian thought, his lips twisting into a cruel smile. Well, Klykka was certainly wasting no time in making a pet out of him. Bloody fucking hell.

The warriors led him toward a large boulder that was currently being guarded by twelve more warrior women. The guards waved their party through, allowing them passage into the tunnels that lay in wait on the other side of the huge rock.

Julian missed nothing as they continued on, his mind noting every curve and pathway they took for future reference. He would escape, he silently vowed to himself.

It didn't matter that his captor was more beautiful than any woman he could have invented in his wickedest, most fevered dreams. He would be no woman's slave.

Not now. Not ever.

Chapter Four

Julian spent the next two hours being bathed, groomed, perfumed and then, finally, oiled down. He sighed, wondering how his life had gone from one extreme to the other in a blink of an eye. One minute he'd been on a men's retreat in the woods getting in touch with his inner animal and a tumble down a hillside later he'd become that animal as he'd ran like marked prey from a hunting party.

And now here he lay, still in chains, watching as four women warriors oiled up his naked body like some exotic pet. That he'd masturbated whilst envisioning scenarios such as this one didn't signify. It was degrading in the extreme when happening in reality.

"He's ready," one of the warriors mused. She ran a finger down his shaft. "His cock is stiff and glistening. The head looks ripe for the plucking."

"Aye," a second warrior confirmed. "Her Worthiness will be pleased with her chattel on this the moon-rising of their wedding."

Julian's breathing stilled. Their…*what?*

"He didn't know," the first warrior speculated. Her forehead wrinkled as she regarded her comrade. As usual, they paid him no attention, treating him as though he was below their notice, even though they had to have been paying him some amount of attention if they were aware of the fact he hadn't realized he'd been forcibly wed to his captor. "What manner of creature is he that he did not know why he was purchased?"

Her comrade waved that away. "All males are slow-witted of the mind. It matters not their species." She sighed like a martyr, causing Julian to frown. "'Tis a boggle why the goddess decreed that we must mate with them in order to birth females. A foul lot, that."

"Now wait a bloody moment!" Julian gritted out. "I am not slow-witted nor will I ever—"

"Think you such a creature as this can please Her Worthiness indefinitely?" a third warrior inquired. She shivered. "I daresay he'll be gulch beast food outside of a fortnight. The poor, pathetic thing. I nigh unto feel sorry for him."

Julian glared at the one lamenting his alleged fate.

"Aye," another one conjectured. "Males are too slow of the head to hold a High Mystik's attention o'er long. He would have been better off as marriage chattel to a lesser female than the Gy'at Li. Soon Her Worthiness will regret what she has done and seek to sever the ties that bind them."

"Through death," the warrior oiling up his chest intoned in a disinterested voice. "'Tis the only way to rid herself of one so unworthy."

Julian frowned. He didn't like the sound of that. Worse yet, if what they were saying was true, he doubted any of them would help him to escape. They were discussing his impending execution as calmly as the weather. Apparently it held no greater import either.

"Our work is done here, warriors." They stood in unison. "Let us deposit the creature in Her Worthiness' chamber and call it an eve."

Julian offered them no resistance as they pulled at his chains to get him to stand. His mind was elsewhere, his every thought on how he might escape.

In the matter of a few minutes he had gone from thinking he was a slave to discovering he had been made into some odd manner of husband to realizing his fate would have been more secure as a slave. Or, at least, he would have had more time to concoct an escape as a slave without the threat of impending death hanging over his head like the blade of a guillotine.

His eyes narrowed in concentration as he was led from the harem chamber. He had kept his gaze alert during the trek to the palace and already knew which route he would take to flee on foot. Now it was merely a question of when.

Chapter Five

Julian was led into a decadent bedchamber big enough to fit a house in. The posh black crystal room was regally decorated with extravagant-looking silk scarves reminiscent of how a sultan's boudoir back on Earth no doubt looked.

A woman—Klykka—was seated on the far side of the room on a throne of sorts, her body discarded of all clothing, even the flimsy G-string she'd once worn. Her legs were spread wide open, glistening pink flesh exposed for all to see, her mons shaved of its black curls. An erect male servant stood stoically to either side of her, staring straight ahead, both of them holding trays of foodstuffs she appeared to be sampling of.

Julian's gaze strayed toward her pussy. It was ripe and lovely, the pinkish-red flesh framed by a caramel-colored body. He shifted uncomfortably on his feet, glancing away as his penis began to stiffen.

"Greet your Lady properly," one of the warriors whispered to him. "Do not play coy as so many Galian husbands would. 'Tis not a worthy attribute to the Gy'at Li."

Julian blinked. He had no idea as to what she was talking about. "I beg your pardon?"

"Go on, virgin," the warrior whispered again, "Greet her rather than wait for her summons. 'Tis a way to start off on her good side." She nodded, her expression serious. "Leastways, I do not believe all males are weak of the mind as many warriors believe them to be. Do not prove me wrong, creature. Greet your Lady."

He frowned. He had no intention of being cooperative but curiosity overwhelmed him. "How precisely does she want to be greeted?"

When the warrior stared at him as though he was an idiot, he decided she'd probably already grouped him in with the rest of the males who were "weak of the mind". So be it. Let her believe that. If everyone thought him a fool, escape would be that much easier.

The warrior huffed, her demeanor impatient. "Get on your knees before the Gy'at Li and pay homage to her cunt."

Julian's body stilled. Depraved, depraved, *bloody* depraved fantasies.

He could only stare at her, his face devoid of all expression. "What am I to do whilst there?"

What a brilliant question! You needn't make yourself appear that stupid.

His face colored when the warrior stared at him as though he had manure for brains. He was beginning to think that wasn't far off from the truth. "What I mean," he gritted out, "is — am I to use my, uh…" He coughed. "Or my, uh…"

The warrior rolled her eyes. "Press your lips to her clit, virgin. 'Tis for a certainty I hope you can do it right. Remember the gulch pits, creature, and suck her cunt as though your pitiful life depends on it. Leastways, it just might."

Julian frowned down at her. "One can only hope that during times of war the job of boosting the morale of the troops doesn't fall to you."

"Eh?"

"Never mind."

He mentally waved away their conversation, his mind focusing on how best to proceed. The defiant part of him wished to stand here and do nothing, to wait until he was forced into "greeting" Klykka. But the practical side of him scoffed at that, for he knew it made more sense to ingratiate himself to his alleged wife until he had time to devise an escape.

His first wife had never allowed him to touch her. This wife apparently wanted him to do nothing but.

Julian's gaze slowly flicked toward the High Mystik, zeroing in on her pussy.

He wished she were ugly. It would have been easier to fool himself into believing that he didn't want to know what she tasted like if her face was riddled with hairy warts and her mouth overrun by rotted teeth. It would have been easier to force himself into believing that what he was contemplating doing was born of sheer force and no will.

Bloody, bloody, *bloody* hell.

Every cell of Julian's humanity played tug-o-war within him. The hungry virgin screamed to be let loose, whilst the refined viscount raged against his sexual side, demanding dignity and freedom in a world that gave men neither. In the end, he did what he knew he had to do.

Julian walked up to Klykka and went to his knees before her. He could smell the sweet, pungent scent of her arousal and damn if it didn't make his cock swell even more. Her pussy was gorgeous. Plump, pink lips, intoxicating scent.

His defenses were crumbling. What was happening to him?

Bloody hell.

He slowly pressed his lips to her engorged cunt. Her breath caught in the back of her throat. Emboldened, Julian's tongue darted out and snaked around her clit, drawing it into the heat of his mouth. She moaned in response, the sound heady. He began to gently suckle her, his lips and tongue tugging at her clit.

"Mmmmm," Klykka purred. "That feels wondrous."

Julian brought his hands up to her pussy and used his fingers to spread the lips apart. The warrior women in attendance gasped in unison, letting him know that he wasn't supposed to touch her. Too bad.

"What are you doing, chattel?" Klykka warned. "Do not think to touch me until I permit—*ooohhhhhh!*"

Spreading her cunt wide open with his hands, Julian dove between her legs and worshipped her clit in long, hard sucks. She moaned, her hips bucking up. He teased her with his tongue, flicking the bud several times in rapid succession before enveloping it in his mouth and suckling again.

"Oh my goddess!" Klykka wailed, her breathing coming in short gasps. "Harder! More!"

Julian nuzzled her cunt like a dog would a bone. He could tell that she was about to burst. Indeed, strange as it was, he could feel her impending orgasm as though it were his own. His eyes widened as he sucked on her clit.

He didn't know how it was possible, but knew with all certainty that when she came, he would too.

"Aye," she gasped. "Oh — *mmmm.*"

Klykka came on a loud groan, her hips bucking up, her legs wrapping around his head. Julian moaned into her cunt as a violent orgasm ripped through him, cum erupting out of his cock and spilling on the ground. Klykka continued to groan, using her sculpted legs to pull his face tighter against her pussy, her entire body shaking until she was replete.

He waited to move until her legs fell from off of him, limp. Assured that she had been completely satisfied, he took to his feet and towered over her. Heart pounding and breathing heavy, he let his gaze wander over the length of her body, noting how hard and erect her pink nipples were.

It was difficult to believe, but he had totally satisfied a woman on the first try. Bloody hell. He should be thankful for porn videos and sex books. Perhaps being a connoisseur of them back home would finally pay off and keep him well away from the death sentence for a while.

Their gazes clashed and the strangest sense of completion stole over Julian. It was an unexpected and, to be sure, unwanted, feeling. The sensation told him that they were meant to be together, that the gods had created Klykka for Julian and Julian for Klykka.

No.

That could never be, would never be. A man couldn't find happiness with a woman who insisted he was chattel.

"Let me go," Julian ground out, his gaze searing. "I want to leave. Now."

He could scarcely credit the notion, but the woman had the temerity to look hurt. What was worse, he could feel her hurt as though it was his own. His heart ached as he stared at her, not understanding the first bit of what was happening to him.

"'Tis not possible," Klykka said, standing up. "You're mine, creature, regardless of whether or not you wish to be."

Her words were biting, but her tone was sad. "Leave us alone, guards." She waved a regal hand. "Away with you the soonest."

Chapter Six

Klykka had never expected to feel anything beyond lust for her chosen husband. She had heard stories of what 'twas like when a wench found her true mate, but none could have prepared her for the depth of those emotions. She had yet to bed him, to bond her to him, and already her body was tense with foreign sentiments.

Love. Need. Completion. Elation. Happiness. Sorrow should she and the creature be parted...

Rarely did a wench, let alone a High Mystik, find her true mate. She wasn't certain if her discovery was a blessing or a curse.

"I cannot say I understand what it is you do to me, creature," Klykka lectured, pacing back and forth naked. "But I will not tolerate it. Nay, I cannot. One such as myself has no time for idle emotions and vacuous sentiments."

"Firstly," he ground out, "my name is Julian. Not 'creature', not 'chattel', nor any other horrid term you devise."

She stopped pacing and stared open-mouthed at him. Nobody talked to her like that. Ever.

"Secondly, *I* am the injured party here!" His chin thrust up with righteous indignation. "I am the one who was kidnapped, chained, woman-handled, married against my will, then brought here to live an utterly meaningless existence as some manner of hired stud!"

73

"You were bought, not hired."

"Arrrrrrrrg!"

The longer she watched him, the more riveting she found him. Other than the male warriors of Trek Mi Q'an, she'd never heard tell of such demanding and commanding creatures as this one. The males of Galis were a sensitive, emotional lot. They cried easily and nigh unto feared their own shadows. They were, in a word, dull.

"I demand to be let go," Julian announced. He nodded, emphasizing his bizarre order. "I wish to return to Earth and carry on with my life." His glower was severe. "My world may be lonely and boring and monotonous and lacking in all ways important, but at least it is, in fact, *mine.*"

So he was from Earth. That tiny little backwater planet in the first dimension? At last it all made sense. The man was but a primitive. Leastways, he was from a time and place where men ruled instead of wenches. 'Twas why he behaved the way he did. Goddess, she had herself a much-coveted and rarely captured primitive! Her wedding day kept getting better and better.

Klykka waved a hand. "Go then."

He stilled.

"Go on. Leave me. I set you free — Julian."

"You, uh…you do?"

"Aye."

Why not? Let him learn the hard way what it meant to be mated. 'Twas, mayhap, the only way a thick-skulled primitive could learn.

"Well," he sniffed. "I thank you for being reasonable. I shall take my leave."

"Go then."

Julian frowned and turned to walk away. Klykka stilled, wondering if true mates behaved the way they were supposed to when one of the mates in question was naught but a primitive.

"Oh my God!" Julian bellowed. His nostrils flared as he turned around to face her. "You've put some manner of spell on me, haven't you? You're letting me leave because you know I can't, aren't you?" He clapped both hands to his forehead. "I'm doomed. Doooooomed!"

Klykka sighed, but had to crack a smile. "I've done nothing of the sort, feisty one. 'Tis just the way of the goddess. 'Tis life when you find your true mate."

"What in the bloody hell does that mean?" he gritted out.

"It means that we are mated for life. It means that should you run from me, your world will become black and your existence meaningless." She walked slowly toward him, then reached out and ran a hand over his chest. "Without me, you are nothing."

His back went rigid. "I suppose I'll just have to take my chances."

"Fine. But remember that you can never know the bed-furs of any wench but I." She shrugged. "Your cock will explode does it taste of another."

He gasped.

"Now that part *is* a spell. And a bedamned good one, I might add."

"You are evil." He pushed her hand away and turned to walk away again. "Horribly, insufferably evil."

Julian made it to the bedchamber door before he let out a guttural cry and began to pant. Clearly he thought to rage against the emotions that had enveloped him.

"Julian?" Klykka said softly. "Are you all right?"

He said nothing.

She moved closer, laying a gentle hand to his back. "All will be well."

"I feel like I'd rather jump off a cliff than be parted from you," Julian said, his voice defeated. "I don't comprehend this, nor do I want it."

Her pride smarted despite herself. "I told you that without me you would be nothing." She could feel his back muscles tense beneath her palm. "'Tis the way of the goddess."

"Well I don't like it."

"After all that you've said to deter me, I can't say that I do either at this moment."

"Then release me from your spell."

Her sigh was soft. "'Tis not a spell, handsome one. 'Tis the way of true mates in this dimension of time and space."

He snorted at that. "So I am nothing without you."

"Nay, you are not." She closed her eyes. "But then neither am I anything without you."

He stilled. She opened her eyes.

Julian slowly turned around and stared down at her. "You feel as badly as I do when I walk away?"

"Aye."

"Like you want to die?"

"Aye."

"Like you'd rather chew broken glass than not have me in your sight?"

"Aye."

"Like you'd rather eat feces and—"

"*Julian.*" She nodded, conceding to whatever horrid mental picture he had almost completed. "Aye."

He tested her words. Julian took three large steps backward. Klykka's violet eyes instantly dimmed, her face a mask of pain. He took a step toward her and watched her eyes begin to glow, their sparkle further illuminating the closer he got.

Finally, at long last convinced, Julian stood over Klykka and sighed. "What do we do now? Because I feel even wretchedly worse than you do when I walk away."

Her smile came slowly. "We just do what the goddess intended for us to do."

"And that would be?"

"Love each other."

Julian didn't know what to think or how to feel. He'd never been so emotionally overwrought and overwhelmed in his entire life. Nothing made sense here. None of the rules were the same.

It wasn't normal to feel such all-consuming terror and loneliness when separated from a woman you had known for all of a day. Or, at least, it wasn't normal where he came from.

And what of his parents? What would they think when he failed to show for the holidays? They'd grieve for his absence, fearing he'd died. Of course, were he to return, they would but continue to chastise him for his perceived failings as a man, for not taking Letty in hand rather than quietly withdrawing from the situation and permitting her to find her happiness with "The Tongue".

The one unmistakable good that would come from Julian's absence on Earth would be that his younger brother, Colin, would be named the new Viscount Jameson. With all of Colin's passionate political leanings, the legacy of the Jameson name was best served in his sibling's hands.

Bloody hell. As if returning to Earth was even an option. He couldn't take three steps away from Klykka without wanting to slit his own throat.

Women. Maddening on Earth, insufferably maddening on…well, wherever in the hell he was.

"Galis," Klykka provided. "We live on the matriarchal planet of Galis in the Trek Mi Q'an galaxy."

Julian's jaw dropped. "You can read my mind?" *Bloody hell!*

"Nay. Just your emotions." She hesitated. "Did I read them wrong?"

"Nay—No."

Julian stared at Klykka—his *wife!*—as he ran a beleaguered hand over his jaw. She *was* beautiful, incredibly so. And she wasn't turning out to be as terrifically misogynist—or whatever the female version of that term was—as he'd originally thought. He began to pace.

He'd never been so confused, unable to figure out up from down, left from right. He didn't want to stay. He couldn't leave. He couldn't be separated from

Klykka, yet he couldn't live happily in a world where men were of no value beyond breeding.

"We will make up our own rules as we go."

He stopped pacing. He glanced around the chamber they were sequestered in. The harem room. Sweet lord, he could never stomach being part of a harem.

"True mates can lay with none but their other half. I shall never know another male."

Julian's face colored. "Stop reading my wretched mind!"

"Emotions," she corrected.

"Semantics," he muttered. "It amounts to the same bloody thing."

Klykka strode over to where he stood and looked up to him with gentle eyes. "I cannot fathom that which you must be going through, handsome one. And yet can I promise to make you happy in all things, to love you with all of my hearts."

He did a double take at her use of the pluralized word *hearts*. Bloody hell, she was possessed of more than one!

"That's just more hearts to love you with."

"You're doing it again," he ground out.

"'Tis sorry I am." Her chuckle was soft and beautiful. He wished he didn't like the sound of it.

"Do not concern yourself with what cannot be changed," Klykka whispered. She reached out a hand and began stroking his penis. "Concern yourself with the here and now."

Julian's breath caught in the back of his throat as she cupped his scrotum and gently kneaded. The massage was incredible. His cock thrust upward, rock-hard in the space of a second. His mind felt a jumble, the desire to mate with her momentarily overwhelming the desire to run away from a situation and place he didn't understand.

"Come," she murmured, holding onto his penis as she guided him toward the bed. "Do not deny your Mistress the right to deflower what belongs to her."

He frowned at the delicate description of his virginity, but followed nonetheless. He was but a man, after all. A hungry virgin who finally had a wife who wanted him.

Julian snatched Klykka up into his arms, sweeping her from the ground. She gasped. He smiled.

"Oh my, feisty one." Her violet eyes glowed with love and arousal. It was all so strange and yet his heart thumped pleasurably. "Remind me to say a prayer of thanks to the goddess for bringing you to me after we've finished."

His heartbeat accelerated to a wicked pace as he laid her onto the palatial bed. She forced him to wonder if this was what he'd wanted all along, a love that grew stronger every moment, a love that would never stale or die.

Bloody hell. Now his thinking was becoming as flowery as her descriptions of him.

"Cease the emotional prattle," Klykka sighed dreamily. "Bind me to you."

Having never been this close to a naked, compliant woman, Julian had to sit back on his knees and stare at her gorgeous pussy and tits. He massaged them as he stared, unable to keep his ravenous hands off her. She was beyond anything, better than any airbrushed centerfold could ever hope to look.

"Julian…"

He came down on top of her, palming her breasts and sucking her nipples. She moaned in response, her hips bucking up, letting him know she wanted filled. But he wasn't done exploring.

Julian tasted her everywhere—her nipples, her cunt, her navel, her arse—everywhere his tongue could find warm flesh. The more he licked, the more bonded to her he felt.

"Julian."

His breathing heavy, Julian settled his cock at the entrance to her pussy and palmed her breasts. His thumbs massaged her nipples as he stared down into her violet eyes.

"Now," she breathed out. *"Please."*

He entered Klykka's cunt on a loud groan, her exquisitely tight flesh accepting him inside. He buried himself to the hilt in one thrust, every muscle in his body tense with need.

He rode her hard, glutting himself on her pussy, penetrating harder and deeper with every thrust. Perspiration-soaked skin slapped perspiration-soaked skin. His teeth gritted with pleasure as he fucked her harder and harder and harder.

"Julian!"

The glow of her violet eyes waxed, their light increasing tenfold. He could tell she was about to come—that he was about to come—and wanted to stave off their climax for as long as possible. She felt so good. Incredibly, sinfully, wickedly good.

He growled like an animal, greedily fucking her pussy, wanting to indulge in the carnal pleasure forever. "You're so tight," Julian ground out, impaling her over and over, again and again and again. His muscles bulged with the strain of trying to hold his cum back. "So damn tight."

Klykka gasped and he knew her orgasm was imminent. He could feel it as though it were his own, magnifying his own impending climax.

"Julian—oh my—Juliaaaaaaaaaan!"

She wailed out her pleasure as a violent orgasm tore through them both. He bellowed from the pleasure, wave after wave of ecstasy engulfing him, the sensations so erotic they were almost painful.

"Klykka."

Julian came again on a thunderous roar as he fucked her pussy faster than a jackhammer. He took her harder and hungrily, greedily fucking her as they both screamed and rode out each delicious wave. They came for what seemed like forever, both of them avariciously accepting all that the other had to give.

When the tide was over, slowly washing away, Julian rolled off Klykka and fell down beside her, panting for air. She snuggled up against him, purring as he put one strong arm around her and held her tightly.

"'Twas wondrous," Klykka whispered.

"Yes, it was," Julian murmured.

He needed to be near her, as close as humanly possible. He didn't comprehend what was happening to him and doubted any of it would make a lick of sense for some time to come.

I love you, Julian.

She didn't say the words aloud, but he could hear them as though she had. They resonated inside of him, warming his cold soul. How could anyone love another in the space of a breath? But she did love him—with more depth and truth than a human could comprehend. And, what's worse, his heart tugged with the same esoteric emotion, unable to stop it any more than he could understand it.

"'Twill be all right," Klykka promised, running a soothing hand over his chest. "These feelings are as new to me as they are to you."

That made him feel somewhat better. Just a little, but it was a start. "Truly?"

"Aye." She smiled. "Leastways, we'll figure them out. Together."

Julian returned her smile. He rarely made the gesture, so he supposed it appeared somewhat awkward.

A vision of things to come stole over him, swamping his senses. He didn't know if Klykka had sent him the visual picture or not, but it was reassuring. Just as she'd promised, they would figure it all out together. He wasn't a slave, would never be a slave. He'd give as good as he got and she'd enjoy every moment of it.

Deep in his heart, crazy as it sounded, he knew that everything would work out just fine. Lord Julian Jameson had once been but a lonely virgin, searching the world of Earth over to find meaning in his life. He'd never found it because it hadn't been there to discover. It had been waiting on him here, galaxies away, in the form of a tiny, beautiful, violet-eyed woman.

"Get some sleep," Klykka grinned. "You'll need it."

Julian's smile came slowly. "Bloody hell. I was hoping you'd say that."

Epilogue

ଞ

"Why do you raise your voice to me?" His bottom lip trembled, threatening another bout of tears. "Have I displeased you, my love?"

"Nay," she said with infinite patience. She smiled as she stroked his face, consoling him. "I could never be displeased with you, little one."

Julian frowned as he watched the incorrigible display from across the dining table. Klykka had invited her sister, Dorra, and Dorra's mate, Vrek, to dine with them. The food was excellent, beyond reproach. But never had a meal dragged out longer.

"Good," Vrek sniffed. "I'm not the kind of boy who should wish to displease his Mistress."

Julian rolled his eyes and looked at a bemused Klykka. If *this* was the typical male on Galis, it was no wonder that the women here thought males inferior to them. Vrek cried at the drop of a hat. Klykka had warned Julian prior to the meal that Vrek's feelings had become extraordinarily hormonal ever since Dorra had become pregnant. Bloody hell. Men here were strange.

Julian sought out his wife's hand and held it. They shared a smile.

Other than meals like this one, the last fortnight with Klykka had been wonderful. Words couldn't begin to describe just how well the two of them fit together. They

made sense in a world that made very little, at least to
Julian.

A warrior entered the dining hall, clearing her
throat. "I fear I must interrupt, Your Worthiness. My
apologies."

Klykka glanced up and used her free hand to wave
her permission. "Speak freely, Ginion."

The warrior nodded. "The empress requests
permission to land on Galis, Mistress."

"The empress?" Klykka's eyebrows shot up. "As in
the High Queen of Tryston?"

"Aye."

"Is she alone?"

"Nay. She is accompanied by three Trystoni females
and three Wani warriors."

Klykka sat back in her chair, seemingly intrigued.
"They no doubt came in search of Dari and Kari who left
here some time ago. But *alone*? 'Tis unlikely the emperor
would allow his wife to travel without his escort. Surely
'tis not the empress, but a lowly imposter."

"We scanned the aircraft they hover above Galis in,
Your Worthiness. 'Tis the empress for a certainty. May
we open the planet's shield for them and allow them
entrance?"

Klykka sat silent, lost in her thoughts. A sense of
foreboding settled over Julian, a feeling he realized came
straight from his wife's emotions. He held her hand
tighter, wondering what had her so concerned.

"Mistress?" Ginion asked. "Do you grant your
permission?"

"Aye," Klykka murmured. "Of course."

GUIDE TO TREK MI Q'AN

ဆ

Contents

ഌ

From the Desk of Jaid Black:
How The Empress Launched an Empire

April 23, 2007 A.D. (Anno Domini)

ജ

November 2007 will mark the seventh anniversary of both Trek Mi Q'an and, because of that distant galaxy, Ellora's Cave Publishing. While I've written dozens of fiction novels and novellas since the day the first book in the series, *The Empress' New Clothes,* was published, Trek Mi Q'an (pronounced Treck Mee Khan) will always hold a special place in my heart. Every author's name is, after all, synonymous with the book or series of books they breathed life into, and those which their readers cherish the dearest. From the beginning, the names "Jaid Black" and "Trek Mi Q'an" have gone hand in hand.

When my publisher, Raelene Gorlinsky, approached me with the idea of writing an introduction for this book, I was very willing but not exactly sure what to write about. After much thought, I decided to go back to the beginning, to explore what was going through my head all those years back when I first started writing *Empress…*

I was in college at the time, an avid romance reader who was giving some serious consideration to a career in anthropology. While my interest in becoming an anthropologist lasted only until I found out I'd have to do excavation work under gross conditions to obtain my doctorate (not this diva!), my fascination with cultural differences — especially sexual ones — continues into the present. That scientific enthrallment is what molds the campy, irreverent, seemingly far-fetched universe of Trek Mi Q'an.

For instance, the opening scene in *No Escape* typically brings me a lot of amused reader feedback, but did you know that there really are females in some matriarchal African tribes who pack-hunt husbands? In one particular tribal nation, when a woman's eye is caught by a good-looking piece of man-flesh, she and her sisters will band together, chase the male down like prey, hit him over the head and drag him (literally) to the altar.

In *No Fear*, Jek and Brynda make their way to Wassa, an underwater world where fish-men rule. Brynda is stunned when they visit a pub wherein the waitresses cover their private parts with food, lie down and welcome the clientele to lick the food from their bodies. As naughty as such a scenario sounds, it really happens in modern-day Japan and has caught on in other parts of the world. (At the time *No Fear* was written, such eateries existed only in Japan.)

For being such a short novella, *Dementia* has always brought me an inordinate amount of reader mail. Women LOVE the gorilla men! I'm not surprised, though, because from a psychological perspective, Dementian males represent the most primal, powerful part of manhood. You Tarzan, me Jane. *Grrrrrrr*.

There is, of course, no denying the parallels between the harems of Tryston and the harems found in modern and historic Arabic culture. While I doubt most women would want to live forever after in such an arrangement, the ménage aspects are—at least until the hero and heroine fall in love—undeniably titillating.

While some of the sexual mores of the various cultures of Trek Mi Q'an are based on the matings of real people, many times they are just made up. For example, I don't think there are any tribes were women are led around naked on leashes by their mates à la Joo, but I could be wrong. (At least I hope that doesn't really happen.)

At any rate, I've been digressing. Back to the late 1990s…

I wrote *The Empress' New Clothes* freestyle, meaning I had no idea what was going to happen until it happened. The only thing I was sure about was that the heroine, Kyra, would be a modern-day human woman thrust into an alien culture with foreign sexual habits. She would learn the shocking ways of the Trystonni world as each new sensual encounter presented itself. Kyra would be given no warning of anything—she would learn it by experiencing it. (I chose the name Kyra after seeing Kevin Bacon's wife of the same name on TV.)

I couldn't seem to write fast enough. The pages whizzed by as I had fun watching her complete her journey. I had expected that Kyra's adventure would be the only time I ever visited the Trek Mi Q'an Galaxy so I wasn't sure what to do when a reader named Giselle kept hounding me for a sequel. In the end I chose to write another story called *No Mercy*. And I thought to myself, "Giselle. Hmm. What a nice name for a heroine…"

From there on out, all of my heroines in the series were named after readers, family and friends. To this day I have a large backlist of reader names I hope to give to some warriors in the future. ☺

Despite the fact that by now reader mail was coming in daily, I still had difficulty accepting that anyone was really reading my work or particularly cared if I ever wrote another sequel. My wake-up call came the first time I received a fan letter from a famous person. She was—is—a tennis star and she wanted me to write a story for Geris, which I later did in *Seized*. And then came a letter from a famous singer via her manager. And then another singer wrote; she needed more to read between gigs. And then an actress. And then another actress's very demanding mother.

Okay, so by the time I got to the exceedingly trying mama bear of a then-famous TV star who has since disappeared into obscurity, I learned two things—one, I might be on to something here with this series, and two, I needed to remove my email address from the public domain because tempestuous mama bears and quality writing time do not go hand in hand. She kept insisting between expletives that I explain to her how the magical sands of Tryston worked to form the Kefa slaves. I finally told her, and this is practically verbatim, "Look, bitch, do you see the word *magical* in there? Well the sands are *magical*. That means I don't have to explain the science behind it because there isn't any. It's *magical*. Magi-fucking-cal. Now go give your daughter a nervous breakdown and leave me the fuck alone." Apparently she did, because I haven't seen Daughter-of-Psycho on TV since. Poor girl. Nor have I heard from mama bear again. Of course, I changed email addresses that day and kept my new one private. I was brought up in the *kick-their-ass-then-run* school of social interaction. Hey, I'm not stupid. They might get back up.

And so a few sequels and a near breakdown later, I felt that a series had been born. Right now I am currently embroiled in writing the final saga of Trek Mi Q'an, at least for the first generation of Trekkies. Until then, peace be unto you.

Jaid

The Evolution of Empress

ℬ

The current version of *The Empress' New Clothes* isn't *quite* the same as the original. As you can see, the cover has evolved. And then there's the "Which chapter should be first?" issue...

2000

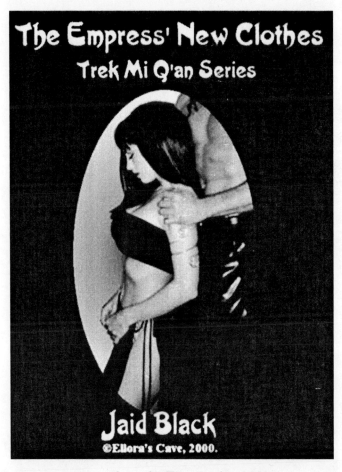

Cover by Tina Engler, 2000

2001

Cover by Daio, 2001

2002

ELLORA'S CAVE PRESENTS

Jaid Black

The novel that took the internet by storm. Recognized by Romantic Times Magazine as a reader's favorite in women's erotica...

The Empress' New Clothes

Cover art by Darrell King, 2002

2005

ELLORA'S CAVE PRESENTS

The novel that took the
internet by storm. Recognized
by *Romantic Times Book Club*
Magazine as a reader's favorite
in women's erotica...

Jaid Black

The Empress'
New Clothes
Trek Mi Q'an: Book 1

Cover art by Darrell King, 2005

About Jaid Black

ဢ

Because inquiring minds want to know – and keep asking.

Q: Where do you get your ideas from?

A: I have no clue. Like the sands from which the Kefa slaves are created, it's a magical process. (Take that, mama bear.)

Q: Are you married?

A: Yeah. Very happily so. Why? You proposing?

Seriously, I don't get why people always want to know if I'm married. I think they feel relieved or something. Like if I was single I must be a horny nut-job, but since I'm married I'm allowed to be a horny nut-job. Double standards, people. Double standards. I'm a horny nut-job no matter my marital status.

Q: What do you look like?

A: I usually get this question from creepy old men. I guess it's the written equivalent to the crank caller's "What are you wearing?" inquiry. The answer I have for all the creepies out there is this—I AM BUTT-UGLY AND I HAVE MULTIPLE VENERAL DISEASES. To all the non-creepies, my answer is this—I'm average height, long, curly hair, sometimes fat, sometimes less fat, and always a hottie. Once you go fat you never go back, baby. And if you try I will sit on you so you can't go anywhere.

Q: What do you do in your spare time?

A: I don't really have any. With two kids, a writing career, several dogs and a strong, brooding, tattooed-from-head-to-toe husband who turns into a whining wuss if I don't pay him enough attention, my days are quite full. (My husband's nickname is BHB—Big Hairy Baby.)

Q: Are you as obnoxiously funny in real life as you are in your books?

A: Yes.

Q: Do you get a lot of people asking you for sexual advice?

A: Yeah, I do. So much so that you'd think the covers of my books read "Masters & Johnson" instead of "Jaid Black". Use a cucumber. Hell, I don't know.

Q: How come you do so few book signings?

A: The answer is pretty blunt and cold—because I hate them. I love my readers, you see. Love, love, love 'em! But my nerves can't handle all the anticipatory anxiety associated with public appearances. I'm a very behind-the-scenes kind of girl so thrusting me into a situation where I have to be the object of attention isn't exactly my idea of a good time. Truth be told, I have to take a Xanax just to get through a signing. Pretty sad, huh? Boy, do I suck. Thanks. Now I'm depressed. I need a cookie.

The Mind Behind Trek

ം

Ellora's Cave put erotic romance on the map. But at the root of this sexy empire is one woman who dared to think differently. Jaid Black answers a few questions about the mind behind Trek and what makes it tick.

Is the goddess the Trystonnis worship named after a real person?

Aparna is a real person. She's my oldest friend — we've been friends since age ten. She is presently a physician and lives in the northeast.

Did you name Khan-Gor after the John Norman sci-fi books based on the planet Gor?

I guess there really is no such thing as an original idea because I'd never even heard of that series of books until reviewers started making comparisons. I read the first Gor book afterwards to see how many similarities there were, but besides the word "Gor" in "Khan-Gor" I still fail to see them.

You do diverse cultures with diverse sexual customs. You do elaborate world-building and complex characters. But one of your trademarks seems to be a taste for the dark and brooding. From many of the Trek planets — like Dementia, which also gets its own title — to a lot of other Trek titles — *No Escape, Seized, No Way Out* — there's a theme of foreboding. Where do you get the inspiration for that darkness, that sense of danger?

I don't know if I'd call it "inspiration" so much as it's simply the way I like to tell a story. I think the more dangerous and forbidden the fruit appears on the outside, the sweeter the nectar becomes inside. ;-)

Do you think Tryston is more like Earth than it might seem at first, only without the attempts to appear "politically correct"?

The warriors of Tryston are not a violent race of men. They feel it is their duty to restore order where it isn't and prevent future chaos from erupting in the seventh dimension of time and space. It was stated in *No Fear* that the cultures that worship the female goddess (for example, Tryston) are the least violent of the races, the cultures that worship male deities are the most volatile and those that worship gods and goddesses of both genders fall somewhere in the middle.

But if you really stop and think about modern day Earth, the parallels can't be mistaken. Damn near all the wars on our planet are caused by men who worship opposing male gods.

You say you've drawn inspiration from real-life friends and foes for some characters, but are there any who go the other way? Any characters you really wish were real? How about ones you love to hate?

The only one that comes to mind is Lord Death. He wasn't supposed to be anyone special, just another secondary character who provided opportunity for a few one-liners. But from the beginning he took on a life of his own and at the end of the day his story will be the most provocative of them all. I'm almost afraid to write his story because I don't know what paths he plans to take me down.

And do you ever find yourself having to hold back on a particular character, scene or plot because it's just getting too intense or crazy?

Definitely. Kyra and Kil's relationship is a good example of that.

Other than the obvious (variety of worlds, opportunity for conflict, complex infrastructures), what are some examples of the appeal of creating a whole universe like Trek Mi Q'an instead of just a single planet? Is it the greater feeling of escape? The craving for omnipotence? The inability to make up your mind?

A little bit of everything? ☺

Seriously, all of us are guilty of omnipotent desires to some extent or another. Whether it be playing God, judge and jury in the Middle East or supporting the death penalty, it's human nature to want to control those things we feel are least controllable. What we can't control scares us. We don't want to think about it or contemplate it, just end it. I'm not saying that's right, in fact I'd say that fundamental truth accounts for the darkest part of the human psyche, but it *is* in all of our natures.

In *The Empress' New Clothes*, the foci were on Tryston and its satellite moons. I began expanding the universe—and thus my artificial omnipotence—after meeting Giselle, the woman I named the heroine after in *No Mercy*. Giselle's life story touched me profoundly and I couldn't shake off the desire to give her a happy ending, at least in fiction. Without revealing too many details of her private life, let's just say that Gis is a brain cancer survivor and has some physical problems that stem from it. She was also responsible for her ailing, aging parents and so rarely got to go anywhere. I gave Giselle a fun, sexy adventure in *No Mercy* and I put her in a dimension of time and space where people live hundreds and thousands of years, where illness is curable and where men love their women faithfully and completely.

What was your inspiration for the characteristics of a Trystonni pregnancy?

Well, seeing as how women on Tryston are only pregnant for a couple of months, I think the inspiration for that one is obvious! On Earth, I found pregnancy to be far less than "glowing", as it's so often described. My ankles swelled up, I felt bigger than Dom Deloise at an all-you-can-eat buffet, and I was pretty sure my kids would never come out. I carried my youngest daughter for what seemed forever, especially considering I was at my biggest during the sweltering heat of a Florida summer. Had she stayed in much longer, she would have come out with a college diploma in hand.

You seem to be pretty dead-set on monogamy as the end result of your main characters' relationships. Sure, there are plenty of luscious ménage scenes in the Trek stories, but ultimately there's one hero and one heroine. Do you think it was purely a product of the time, since you were already pushing the envelope on so many things and erotic romance had yet to catch on, let alone permanent ménage stories? Or is it more about your personal tastes—at least in romance?

This is a really good question and one I've never before been asked. I'd have to say it was a lot of both. First, when I wrote *Empress* ménages were not, as you indicated, even remotely acceptable in the romance genre. There came a point in the story where I had to make a choice as to whether Kyra would have intercourse with Kil or not. My hormones screamed yes, but the monogamist in my heart screamed no. It was a very difficult decision, but not unlike the choices real women face daily. Ultimately, as sexy and risqué as sex outside of marriage can seem, I'm a strong believer in fidelity and intimacy between two people, whatever their genders or orientation. You never see love triangles work out—ever. I defy you to show me even one long-term example!

How long did it take you to write Empress? Did you find it got easier or harder to write later stories as the series got longer and more in-depth?

I wrote *Empress* very quickly. I'd say it only took me about two months at best. It got much harder to write stories as the series went on. I think I've put off the remaining stories in the series for as long as I have because of a fundamental laziness on my part. I enjoy writing, not fact-checking!

Your portrayal of the Smiling Faces and Peaceful Hearts Meditation Retreat in *Empress* is charming and funny, and it's a very effective foil to the major change of scenery Kyra and Geris are about to experience. And the retreat helps most of the characters, Lord Jameson notwithstanding. (On second thought...) But do you think we as humans need a little healthy shaking up— even if it's not as extreme as what our Earth-born heroines get—as much as we need serenity and relaxation?

Absolutely. I get bored when things become routine, no matter how pleasant and uneventful such a situation is. We need yin as much as yang and vice versa.

As you've hinted before, Empress is about more than sex and romance—it's about diversity. Along with the hot fantasies and a vivid alternate universe, are you

offering your readers a gentle suggestion to keep an open mind?

The point of the entire series is that beauty is in the eye of the beholder. What is considered beautiful in one culture is ugly in another. As women, the greatest gift we can give ourselves is the ability to fall in love with what we see in the mirror every day. That isn't vanity; it's simply — and beautifully — self-love.

Titles in the Trek Mi Q'an Series

Main Series Titles

1   The Empress' New Clothes – *Zor and Kyra*
1.5   Seized – *Dak and Geris*
2   No Mercy – *Rem and Giselle*
3   Enslaved – *Kil and Marty*
4   No Escape – *Kara and Cam*
5   No Fear – *Jek and Brynda*
5.5   Dementia – *General Zaab and Dee*

Related Short Stories

Naughty Nancy – *Nancy and Vorik* [Available in *Strictly Taboo* anthology from Berkley]
Devilish Dot – *Dot and Vaidd* [in *Manaconda* anthology]
Never a Slave – *Lord Julian Jameson and Klykka*

Coming in Future

6   No Way Out: Jana – *Jana and Yorin*
7   No Way Out: Dari – *Dari and Gio*
8   No Way Out: Kari – *Kari and Death*
9   No Way Out: Armageddon

The Planets and Moons

ॐ

Trek Mi Q'an: (pronounced Trek Mee Kwan) The prominent galaxy that exists within a seventh-dimensional plane of being. Literal translation: "Galaxy of Warriors".

Tryston: (pronounced Tri-sten) The ruling planet of Trek Mi Q'an galaxy, the principal seat of the Emperor, and the principal seat of the High King. Tryston is on the far edge of Trek Mi Q'an galaxy.

Morak: The dominant satellite moon of Tryston; home of King Kil, second-born son.

Ti Q'won: (pronounced Tee-Kwan) The fifth closest moon to Tryston; a general name for the habitable part of the fifth moon; home of King Dak, the third son.

Sypar: A satellite moon of Tryston; home of King Rem, the fourth son. King Rem's home is the "Ice Palace", a structure molded from ice-jewels–splinters of ice fused with precious white gems, a development that takes thousands of Yessat Years to occur.

Galis: The only matriarchal planet in Trek Mi Q'an galaxy. Galis is ruled by female Mystiks who are proficient warriors and skilled in the erotic arts.

Myrak: Planet situated between Tryston and Galis.

Tron: Planet from which Tron insurrectionists come. The Wani sector (mentioned in *Enslaved* and *No Fear*) is on the planet Tron. Most of the planet has been destroyed by the insurrectionists. High Empress Jana, mother of Zor, Kil, Dak and Rem, was killed by insurrectionists on the planet Tron. The world is tinted blue. The planet has four moons.

Brekkon: Referenced in *No Escape*. The males of this planet are not reputable or reliable.

Kampor: Large planet of dull purple. It has twenty moons. It is fifteen billion years older than Earth. The inhabitants are crude primitives compared to the inhabitants of Tryston, but they are one thousand times more advanced than Earth in biological evolution and technology. Kampor is the planet that Jek points out to Brynda in *No Fear*, when she tries to tell him that her disease is incurable.

Tojo: Large, orange-red planet with a "chilly" atmosphere. Indigenous life includes *pugmuffs* and *Rustians*.

Unnamed Fifth Dimension planet: Referenced in *No Mercy*. A planet inside a wormhole. A treacherous land full of predators, many of which are transparent and fanged. The ground is red and gel-like, sometimes slippery, and covered in a red mist. When Giselle, Rem and the others crash on the planet, the sky is smoky and black. The planet has three suns.

Joo: Sixth dimension planet, close to the penal colony of Trukk. The humans (lusty, naked women, clothed males) have silver and lavender skin tones. The environment of the planet is jungle-like and the sky is filled with purple haze. The natives of the planet tend to live underground. The towns of Treeka (where women can't have money and instead barter with oral sex) and Lii-Lii (where women can wear no clothing and must be leashed) are on this planet.

Zolak: Vakki sector of this planet is ruled by King Jun, son of High King Zor and High Queen Kyra. The sector is practically nonexistent after insurrectionist occupation.

Zideon: Home of Cam K'al Ra.

Khan-Gor: "Planet of the Predators", a supposedly mythical planet of barbarians in the Zyrus Galaxy of the seventh dimension. Legend has it that the inhabitants of the planet, humanoid creatures who can take a gargoyle-like shape they call *"kor-tar"*, closed off the planet in response to the rest of the galaxy's fear of them. The planet is silver-toned and icy cold. The barbarians live in Clan strongholds. There is no monetary system on Khan-Gor, the inhabitants barter the low-intellect beings called *yenni*.

Kabka star system: Star system in the third dimension with four suns. Referred to in No Fear as "a hell", Kabka is a hostile environment with primitive, violent inhabitants.

Wassa: The outlying planet in the Kabka star system in the third dimension. Wassa is small, no bigger than Europe on first-dimension Earth, and is frigid. The daytime is arctic, but there is no snowfall. The inhabitants of Wassa, fish-like humanoids, live underwater. The planet is lime-green, the waters blue. The slave trade is booming on Wassa but the planet is primarily peaceful. They worship a goddess.

Dementia: The second farthest from Kabka's four suns, Dementia is inhabited by violent, gorilla-like humanoids. The planet is jungle-like and dark and gloomy with red-tinted skies, and is as dangerous as its inhabitants. Carnivorous animals roam freely. Predatory plantlife has been harnessed by the Dementians to aid in breaking their slaves. Native Dementians are male; Dementians only have sons.

Geography of Tryston

ဢ

The planet Tryston is vast, approximately the size of three Jupiters, and possesses seventeen satellite moons. It takes months to travel by floating conveyance from one side of the planet to the other. The geography of Tryston is comprised of three parts — the city centers, the borderlands and the pits.

Throughout Tryston are millions of city centers. A typical city center on Tryston is built around the largest dune of healing sand in any given area. If the city center is also the principal seat of a lesser king's holdings, then the lesser king who rules the area typically lives in a palace that sits at the apex of the dune. The high lords live in strategically placed castles at the bottom of the dune, facing in the general direction of the sectors they rule. There are typically three or four city centers in any given sector.

The majority of Tryston's people, most of them warriors and free men, live within these surrounding centers. It is the function of the warriors to protect the free men of the centers, providing them with security so they can go about their daily business.

Separating the city centers from the pits are the borderlands. The borderlands are comprised of colored sands and little else. The terrain here is harsh and typically uninhabitable.

The pits dot the landscape of Tryston. The black terrain is habitable but severe. Both animal and gel-based predators make their home in pits such as Kogar. When people from Trek Mi Q'an are sentenced to die, they are sent to the pits to fend for themselves.

Royal Lineage

ಐ

Emperor: the warrior who reigns over the entire Trek Mi Q'an galaxy. If he does not have a male heir, he also carries the title of High King.

High King: the warrior who reigns over planet Tryston; the Emperor-apparent.

Empress: the wife of the Emperor; she also carries the title High Queen if she has never borne a son.

High Queen: the wife of the High King; the Empress-apparent.

Grand Empress: the living widow of an Emperor.

King: title given to son of an Emperor; rule vast areas of land, usually entire planets and/or moons.

High Princess: daughter of the Emperor.

Princess: daughter of a King.

High Lord: title given to son of a King; rules sector within a King's kingdom. There are also High Lords who are not related to the royal family but have been given the title by the Emperor.

Chief Priestess: the governing religious ruler of Tryston and Trek Mi Q'an. Also called "Q'i Liko Aki Jiq"—"She Who Is Born of the Goddess". In the event that an Emperor dies without an heir, the Chief Priestess rules Trek Mi Q'an until she appoints the next Emperor and relinquishes power to him. Although mothered by unnatural means, the Chief Priestess is nevertheless a mortal. She is the biological and metaphysical result of a sexual union between the goddess Aparna and a chosen Trystonni male.

Tryston's Ruling Family

ॐ

The deceased Emperor Zal Q'an Tal and the deceased Empress Jana Q'ana Tal begat four sons: Zor, the current Emperor of Trek Mi Q'an; Kil, the king of the dominant moon Morak; Dak, the king of the moon Ti Q'won; and Rem, the king of the moon Sypar.

The Emperor Zor Q'an Tal married the Empress Kyra Q'ana Tal in the year 6023 YY. They begat five daughters and two sons: The High Princesses Zora, Zara, Kara, and Klea; High King Jor; the High Princess Geris; and Jun, the king of Zolak.

King of Morak, Kil Q'an Tal, married the Queen Marty "Mari" Q'ana Tal in the year 6040 YY. They begat two daughters and three sons, the eldest of the children named Princess Zy'an, the youngest of the children named Princess Zoë. The king's heir is High Lord Kilian. His other two sons are High Lord Darif, and High Lord Khan.

King of Ti Q'won, Dak Q'an Tal, married the Queen Geris Q'ana Tal in the year 6023 YY. They begat three sons and three daughters in the following order: Princess Jana, High Lord Dar, Princess Dari, High Lord Zar'an, High Lord Ren, and Princess Hera.

King of Sypar, Rem Q'an Tal, married the Queen Giselle Q'ana Tal in the year 6040 YY. They begat seven sons and one daughter: Their only female hatchling is Princess Zari. Their sons, in birth order, are: High Lords Kilak, Ri'an, Zar, My'ak, Vaz, Ra, and Kalïq.

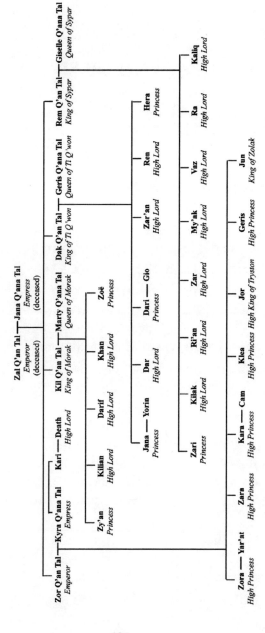

Political Culture

ဢ

Trystonni political culture is central to the Trek Mi Q'an galaxy and is hierarchical in nature. At the apex of the hierarchy sits the Chief Priestess, the most powerful mortal in existence.

Below the Chief Priestess is the Emperor, the ruler of Trek Mi Q'an galaxy.

Below the Emperor is the High King, the ruler of Tryston and the Emperor's firstborn son.

Below the High King are the lesser kings. Lesser kings tend to rule vast areas of land, usually entire planets and/or moons.

Below the lesser kings are the high lords. High lords rule sectors within a lesser king's kingdom.

Equal in stature to the high lords are the priestesses of Tryston. The priestesses report directly to the Chief Priestess but are bound by the Holy Law to defer in all matters to lesser kings, the High King and the Emperor.

Below the high lords and priestesses is the warrior, or military, caste. This caste is responsible for maintaining the tranquility and order of a sector, so there are typically quite a few warriors under the command of a high lord within any given sector.

Below the warrior caste is the caste of free men. The majority of the population is comprised of free men. This class consists of the workers, merchants and craftsmen of the planet.

Below the caste of free men are the bound servants, all female. A bound servant is answerable to any caste above her. She is chattel to whoever owns her during her five years of sexual and physical servitude, and she is not permitted to marry until she is freed. Although, technically speaking, a male of the free caste is permitted to own a bound servant, this is a rare event as her sale price tends to be exorbitant.

Below the bound servants are the Kefa slaves. A Kefa slave cannot be considered a real class as they are not thinking beings. They are made of colored sand, female in form and engineered by magic to do nothing but give pleasure.

The political structure of Trek Mi Q'an is not immobile. A free man, for instance, can move up in caste if his skills as a fighter are remarkable. The only three places on the hierarchy that are impossible to join unless you are born to them are Chief Priestess, Emperor and High King.

Religious Life

ဢ

Just as the planet Tryston dictates political life throughout the Trek Mi Q'an galaxy, so too does it dictate religious life. The religion of the Trystonni people is monotheistic and is based upon the worship of the goddess Aparna.

Aparna very rarely interferes in the lives of mortals. Instead, her wishes are made known through her daughter, the Chief Priestess Ari. If Ari were to die, a moon-phasing would occur, the skies would turn to black and Trek Mi Q'an would be closed off to outsiders until Aparna begat another daughter with a chosen Trystonni male.

Like her omnipotent mother, Ari very rarely interferes in the lives of the people she was born to rule and serve. Although her station in life is higher than the Emperor's, she typically defers to him in all matters except the spiritual.

Ari is the most powerful mortal in existence and is the sole medium between her mother, the goddess Aparna, and lesser mortals. She is served directly by priestesses she chooses.

The religion of Tryston is very sexual in nature. It is believed that higher levels of understanding are reached through higher levels of sexual enlightenment. Hence, healing and social ceremonies almost always contain sexual touching and intercourse.

Glossary

ഉ

Aparna: the dark goddess of war and pleasure, worshipped by all Trystonni.

Bloodmate (see *vorah*): Khan-Gori term for wife.

Boggi: a set of four shackles sometimes used by Galian females to break recalcitrant males.

Bound servant: a sex slave, typically acquired through a war. Bound servants, unlike Kefas, are not slaves for life. They are released after five Yessat Years of sexual and physical servitude. Although they wear the *qi'ka*, the traditional skirt of Trystonni females, their breasts remain unbound, separating them from free women.

Bridal necklace: a crystal necklace with which a Trystonni warrior binds his Sacred Mate to him. Bridal necklaces are individual to each male and are irreplaceable if destroyed. If a Sacred Mate dies the bridal necklace stays locked around her neck even in death. If a false Sacred Mate is given a bridal necklace, upon her death the necklace will unclasp and can be used again. Such is the case for the relationship between Rem and Jera in *The Empress' New Clothes*, with Rem claiming his true Sacred Mate in *No Mercy*. Bridal necklaces have many magical properties, most of which are common knowledge in the Trek Mi Q'an universe. Some of these properties include showing emotion via color, linking life forces between Sacred Mates and language translation. During intercourse, the bridal necklace reflects the pleasure felt between mates and, after the male's orgasm, produces a pleasurable "aftershock" that can cause unconsciousness in extreme cases. Unmated males envy mated males the pleasure brought by the bridal necklace.

Bryyif: silver gun-like mechanism that shoots liquid fire instead of bullets. Used by the female warriors of the Wani sector of Tron. (Referenced in *Enslaved.*)

Cherished One: Dementian endearment. (Referenced in *Dementia.*)

Consummation Feast: an ancient custom that precedes the claiming of a King's Sacred Mate. It is the only time that mated warriors and their Sacred Mates stretch their monogamous bonds. It is a time when women work their warriors to a frenzy of jealousy. Before the ceremony ends, the warriors are brought to a peak by *Kefa* slaves, while Sacred Mates are pleasured to a peak by unmated males.

Credit: the unit of money used in Tryston and on most planets within Trek Mi Q'an.

Dementian vines: indigenous vines of the planet Dementia. They eat vaginal secretions and inject their prey with a euphoric, hallucinogenic drug. While the vine wraps and constrains the victim, the flowers and buds of the plant work on the nipples and clitoris to produce maximum pleasure in the female, thereby maximizing the production of their food at the source. They are used by the natives of Dementia to break their human female slaves, but if not monitored, vines can cause dehydration and insanity. Evidence suggests that the needle-like injectors of the vines are sometimes withdrawn by the plant (as in *No Fear*) or can be distracted by a "fake-flesh box" (as in *Dementia*).

Devolution: metabolic change where Trystonni males revert to a primitive, mindless, savage beasts, or "baser self". The most recognizable sign of devolution is growling, but eye color changes are prominent as well. The Chief Priestess can forestall devolution through healing sex but cannot cure it. The prison of Trykk on the planet Joon in the sixth dimension holds devolved males. Some rationality can occur even in devolved males. (Detailed explanation in *No Mercy*.)

Dreamscape: an opening within the Rah.

Fala: Trystonni numeral referenced in *No Escape*. Represented by a hieroglyphic-like symbol.

Fireberry (also "fire-berry"): fruit of the pici tree.

Gastro-gel: fuel that caused the fires that destroyed Cam's home.

Gazi-kor: beasts referenced in *No Escape*. They go into heat and have metallic skin.

Gel-lamp: used across the galaxy for light.

Gentling: process whereby the female Sacred Mate of the head of a bloodline is introduced to her "lesser husband" and attuned to his touch in case the female's mate dies before a male heir is born and the need arises for the lesser husband to produce an heir with the female. It is a time for the establishment of a relationship. The process involves direct touch of the female's genitals by the lesser husband, but the rules are strict—hands only, no tongue or penis. Some lesser husbands cannot stand the torture and penetration occurs. During the gentling the lesser husband and female to be gentled are locking in a room together. The gentling has no set term of duration, but is ended when the lesser husband is satisfied that the female has been sufficiently gentled.

Giatta balls: a sweet delicacy. Served by Marty at Kil's feast in *Enslaved*.

Gorak: "sleep of the dead." Khan-Gori evolutionary process undergone in between the first through seventh Khan-Gori lifetimes. *Gorak* is undergone once every five hundred YY and involves a male cocooning himself (similar to the females' evolution in a *vorah sac*) for one hundred YY.

Gulch beast: flying predators that live in swamps and trap their prey in "gulch pits". They are seen as "red flashes".

Gulch pit: a trap dug by a gulch beast to trap food.

Haja birds: referenced in *No Escape* — "Kill five *haja birds* with one *trelli* stone."

Hatchling: a post-incubation fetus; a baby. This is also a general term used when referring to one's own children, no matter their age.

Heeka-beast: a beast whose temper Kil frequently compares Marty's to in *Enslaved*. They are reptilian, generally about eight feet tall, and armored with a blue-black substance. They have two hands with five projections, each ending in a twelve-inch razor-sharp nail.

Holo-maze: game often involving betting. Kyra challenges Geris to a game of it in *Enslaved*.

Holo-port: instantaneous transportation that can take a traveler between planets or even dimensions — they step in on one world and step out on another. Evidence (such as in *No Mercy*) suggests that the coordinates of a holo-port are singular and non-changeable.

interact with the world on a plane of reality incomprehensible on Earth as we know it.

Sii: Trystonni numeral referenced in *No Escape*. Represented by a hieroglyphic-like symbol.

Summoning: act of mental compulsion upon objects performed by warrior-kings.

Sweet juice: comparable to human breast milk; blue plasma substance that fills a *mani*'s breasts after her *pani* are born, to nourish the *pani*.

Taka: Dak compares Kyra's nipples to these in *The Empress' New Clothes*.

Taka juice: suggested as an alternative to sweet juice for Kil and Marty's daughter in *Enslaved*.

Tipo: game mentioned in *The Empress' New Clothes*.

Tishi paint: maroon paint used as camouflage by Galian warrior women when hunting in the Trefa Jungle. Referenced in *No Escape*.

Trelli: shimmering, colored sand found in the borderlands of Tryston.

Tu-tu bush: found in the Trefa Jungle on Galis. They frequently have holes near the base of the bush.

Ty'ka (pronounced "tee-kah"): literal translation "my hearts"; a term of extreme affection.

Vazi: "Mommy". Khan-Gori term.

Vesha: an animal indigenous to Tryston that is valued for its silk-like fur. (In *No Escape* the color of the *vesha* hide is described as "rouge".)

Virginity: in Trystonni cultures, virginity is determined by whether or not a woman has had intercourse with a Trystonni warrior. Intercourse with lesser males cannot affect a female's virgin status.

Vorah: Khan-Gori term. Means "wife" or "Bloodmate". Describes the mated female mate of a Khan-Gori Barbarian male, after she has evolved.

Vorah-sac: incubation cocoon where female Bloodmates evolve after being claimed by a Khan-Gori male. Evolution takes one sennight. The *vorah-sac* grows shortly after claiming and is made of sticky, web-like filaments.

Yenni: primitive creature native to the planet Khan-Gor. They are comparably intelligent as a *Kefa* slave of Tryston, run on all fours and have luminescent white skin, black eyes and sharp, icy tails. Males of the species, who subsist on vaginal secretions, run in packs and have designated leaders. Females of the species, who eat life-force (semen) from Khan-Gori males, run in their own packs. Some females are naturally Alpha. *Yenni* serve as the Khan-Gori currency. Males can own *yenni* once they reach eighteen YY of age, and they are an unmated Khan-Gori male's only source of sexual pleasure. In *Devilish Dot*, Dot mistakes a *yenni* mating as a rape.

Yessat Years: the standard measure of time in Trek Mi Q'an; one YY is equal to ten Earth years.

Zahbi: Dementian term for wife or mate. A female is generally not called this unless she is visibly pregnant.

Zorg: leather-like armbands that can detonate various deadly and debilitating weaponry. Can fly the body of a warrior. Created and produced on Ti Q'won.

Zya: "little one". Khan-Gori endearment.

Zykif: a weapon.

Zyon pack: a Barbarian pack on Khan-Gor.

Characters

ɛͻ

Chief Priestess Ari

Name means "Holy One".

Tall, statuesque and blonde, with large perky breasts, puffy pink nipples and a great butt. She is described in *The Empress' New Clothes* as being a dead ringer for Pamela Anderson.

When she meets Kyra, Ari is one hundred Yessat Years old, but she looks eighteen.

Bazi

Nine-Yessat-Year-old boy who escapes the planet Arak with Dari.

Brynda Q'ana Ri (née Brynda Mitchell)

Brynda has blonde hair and blue eyes. She is thirty-six years old when she meets Jek Q'an Ri. Her first husband was named Henry.

Cam K'al Ri

King of Zideon.

Cam has golden hair. In *The Empress' New Clothes* he has green eyes. In *No Escape* his eyes are brilliant turquoise.

Dak Q'an Tal

King of Ti Q'won.

Dak has blond hair and glowing blue eyes. He is over seven feet tall and heavily muscled.

Dari Q'ana Tal

Sacred Mate to Gio Z'an Tar, yet unclaimed.

Death

High Lord of the Jioti Sector

Heavily tattooed ex-convict. He has dark hair, golden eyes and a large skull tattooed on his forehead.

Delores "Dee" Ellison, aka "Scheme"

Mate to Zaab of Dementia.

She is twenty-nine when she is mysteriously brought to the planet Dementia. She has golden hair and blue eyes.

Dorothy "Dot" Arazia

Bloodmate to Vaidd Zyon.

She has doe-brown eyes, chestnut brown hair and large breasts. She is thirty-five years old when she is brought to the planet Khan-Gor and meets her Bloodmate, Vaidd.

Geris Q'ana Tal (née Geris Jackson)

Sacred Mate to Dak Q'an Tal.

Geris is described as "long and sleek" with "flawless mahogany skin". Her best friend Kyra compares her to the Egyptian Queen Nefertiti. She has micro-beaded black hair that falls to the center of her back. Fashionably toned and regally sculpted, she is supermodel-beautiful and has light brown, almond-shaped eyes and full red lips. She takes pride in her hair, which has never been cut and she swears it never will be. She is thirty-two when she joins with Dak.

Gio Z'an Tar

Son of King of Arak. Sacred Mate to Dari Q'ana Tal, daughter of Dak Q'an Tal and Geris Q'ana Tal.

Giselle Q'ana Tal (née Giselle McKenzie)

Sacred Mate to Rem Q'an Tal.

Giselle is from Shoreham, Australia, Earth. When she meets Rem she is a thirty-six-year-old virgin. She is five foot four and has long strawberry-blonde hair, large green eyes and pale, freckled skin. She has two pet poodles, named Byrony and Tess, who accompany her to the seventh dimension.

Jana Q'ana Tal

Deceased.

A native of Tron, Jana was Empress of Tryston and Sacred Mate to Zar Q'an Tal, mother to Zor, Kil, Dak and Rem. She had golden hair and blue eyes.

Jana Q'ana Tal (II)

The daughter of Geris and Dak.

She has golden hair and blue eyes and is the spitting image of her father — and her grandmother.

Jek Q'an Ri

Son of Tia and Jik. Jek was a student of the warring arts under Kil Q'an Tal. He is Sacred Mate to Brynda Mitchell. He has blue eyes.

Kara K'ala Ri (nee Kara Q'ana Tal)

The third daughter of Kyra and Zor.

She has black hair and blue eyes. She was labeled a "mischief-maker" early in life, and is a "twin in spirit" to Dak and Geris' daughter, Jana. During her time on the planet Galis, she was known as "Kara Gy'at Li". She is a proficient hunter/warrior.

Kari Gy'at Li (née Kara Summers)

Sacred Mate to Lord Death, yet unclaimed. Younger sister of Kyra Q'ana Tal, nee Kyra Summers.

Kara disappeared one Earth year before Kyra met Zor. She fell off the Pirates of Penzance ride at Disney World and was never heard from again.

Kil Q'an Tal

King of Morak, High Lord of the Kyyto Sectors and King of Planet Tron.

Kil looks like his father, Emperor Zar. He is the second-oldest brother to Zor, Dak and Rem. He has deep tan skin and is the same height as Zor — seven foot four. He has blue eyes and black hair and a jagged scar across his right cheek.

Kyra Q'ana Tal (née Kyra Summers)

Sacred Mate to Zor Q'an Tal, High King of Tryston and Emperor of Trek Mi Q'an.

Kyra has wine-red hair and a pale, creamy complexion. She has the trademark "Summers eyes" — silver-blue. She is described as having a "full" body and being "lush of hip and breasts". On Earth Kyra was a tax accountant. She is thirty-one Earth years old when she becomes Zor's Sacred Mate.

Mari Q'ana Tal (née Martha "Marty" Matthews)

Sacred Mate to Kil Q'an Tal.

Mari was twenty-one years old when she fell into the river in the commune on Earth and thirty-one when she arrived in the Wani sector of the planet Tron. She has honey-gold hair and gray eyes. During her time with the Wani she earns a blue navel ring and a blue ring in her left nipple.

Nancy Lombardo

Lived in Salem, Massachusetts before being mysteriously transported to the planet Khan-Gor. She has brown eyes and soft amber hair, wears glasses and sometimes contacts. She is the mate of Vorik F'al Vader.

Rem Q'an Tal

King of Sypar, one of Tryston's lesser moons.

Rem is the youngest brother to Zor, Kil and Dak. He has blond hair and blue eyes. His devolution causes his eyes to shift from blue to green.

Ty

Ty was the leader of the Tron insurrectionists. A large man, stocky and sinewy, with a shaved head and a close-cropped beard.

Vaidd Zyon

Heir to the Zyon Pack on the planet Khan-Gor. Bloodmate to Dot.

He is between seven and a half and eight feet tall and has light brown hair with golden streaks. His eyes are silver. He is heavily muscled and a jagged scar zigzags down the right side of his torso.

Vandor

Mate to Zara Q'ana Tal.

He has black hair and vivid green eyes.

Vorik F'al Vader

Son of Yorin, bloodmate to Nancy Lombardo.

Vorik has silver eyes and shoulder-length black hair. He is eighteen Yessat Years old when he meets Nancy.

Yorin

Mate to Princess Jana Q'ana Tal, was a servant on Galis before meeting her. He has silver eyes and black shoulder-length hair.

General Zaab

Alpha Male of the Highlander Mantus Hoard and Supreme Master of the Highlanders. He has green eyes and black hair/fur and is over seven feet tall. He has deadly incisors, but otherwise normal, human-looking teeth.

Zara Q'ana Tal

Daughter of Kyra and Zor. Mate to Vandor, but not yet fully claimed.

Zara is light-hearted and bubbly, flirty and sociable. She has red hair and glowing blue eyes. She is the twin sister of Zora.

Zor Q'an Tal

Name means "The Excellent One".

High King of Tryston, Emperor of Trek Mi Q'an galaxy, Guardian of the Sacred Sands,

Zor has black hair, worn below the shoulders and braided in a series of three rows off his temples. He has blue eyes and golden-brown skin. He is seven foot four and three hundred seventy pounds. He is forty-two Yessat Years old (four hundred twenty years, Earth time) when he marries Kyra.

Zora Q'ana Tal

Daughter of Kyra and Zor. She is the Sacred Mate of Yar'at, though not yet claimed or confirmed.

Zora is sensitive, contemplative and reflective. She has red hair and glowing blue eyes. She is the twin sister of Zara.

Enjoy an excerpt from:
DEATH ROW: THE TRILOGY

Cell Block 29:
Death Row unit within the Kong Penal Colony.
40 miles outside the Mayan pyramidal ruins of Altun Ha
in former Belize, The United Americas of Earth,
December 17, 2249 A.D.

৪৩

"Prisoner, Riley. Remove your clothing."

Kerick Riley's dark head came up slowly, his cold gray eyes flicking dispassionately over the smirking face of the prison warden. Wiping mud from his eyes, he rose up to his feet from the pen of wet dirt and blood he'd been kicked into, simultaneously noting everything there was to see about the executioner. From the pristine white silk robe the warden wore, to the flash-stick in his hand that could ignite and thereby sizzle a man to death at mere contact, nothing escaped his notice.

For fifteen years, seven months, three weeks, and five days, Kerick had waited with an inhuman patience for the arrival of this moment. He'd never allowed his mental acumen or extreme physical strength to lessen from lack of use over the years, that both would be there to serve him when the hour of reckoning had at last come upon him.

It had worked—it *would* work.

Never once in all of those fifteen plus years had he allowed his thoughts to betray him. He knew when it was safe to think, and he knew as well when it was necessary to create a void in his mind to prohibit a detection scanner from probing what went on in his thoughts.

From a young age he had been taught the necessity of control, his mother having gone so far as to beat the lessons into him. She'd used such harsh tactics not because she had hated her son, but conversely because she had adored him, and more fundamentally, because she had wanted him to live.

The lessons in bodily and mental control passed down from Tara Riley had done more than help Kerick survive in the violent world of twenty-third century Earth; they had also made it possible for him to survive this day. Today. The dwindling hours of remaining daylight prior to his execution.

Kerick's sharp gray eyes continued to study the warden, but betrayed none of his emotions. They simply calculated and assessed with an almost robotic precision, doing the same as they'd always done these past fifteen years. He realized that the sadistic warden had always despised—and envied—his ability to think and behave as though he were a machine, for it made predicting his behavior impossible.

Warden Jallor tapped the flash-stick against his thigh, his eyebrows shooting up mockingly. He believed he'd won, Kerick knew, thought indeed that the prisoner was about to die...

But—no.

For nearly every waking moment of the past fifteen years, Kerick had calculated, assessed, plotted, and planned. He had noted the weaknesses of the 50-story structure surrounding him, had made certain that he'd learned all there was to know of the seemingly impenetrable fortress that was his prison. For the most part, he understood that Warden Jallor was correct—Kong was an impenetrable fortress. But Kerick also understood that there was no such thing as invincible, and he had spent fifteen years learning how to defeat the undefeatable Kong.

Officially entitled Correctional Sector 12, the penal colony of Kong had gotten its nickname from an old black-and-white movie none from Kerick's time had ever seen but all had heard tell of. It was said that in the old movie the god-like ape King Kong could escape from any prison, but not even the Mighty Kong could escape Sector 12. For most prisoners, that statement turned out to be chillingly true, but for Kerick Riley...

"Remove your clothes," Warden Jallor snapped, his patience nearing an end. His icy blue eyes flicked down to the innocuous bulge in the prisoner's pants. "Now."

He wanted to kill him. For year after bitter year, Kerick had comforted himself with thoughts of Jallor's death, with thoughts of avenging himself — and avenging his mother. But for the moment at least, such was not to be. He needed the warden alive. For now.

But when it was over, when all was said and done...

Kerick's stoic gaze never wavered from Jallor's as he slowly, methodically, removed first his prison-issued woolen tunic and finally his woolen pants. Both garments were a dirty, muted brown, filthy and greasy from having been worn for three solid years without a cleaning. In truth, removing the disgusting clothing was practically a relief. It would mean he was naked during the escape, but so be it.

When he was finished, Kerick stood before Warden Jallor in stone-faced silence, his heavily muscled six-foot five-inch frame completely divested of clothing, his brooding eyes that saw everything piercing the warden's.

Jallor's gaze wandered down to Kerick's penis, then back up to his face.

He was a stupid man, Kerick knew. Sadistic but stupid. Removing the prisoner from his chains would prove to be his downfall.

With the sensory chains on, Kerick never would have stood a chance at escaping. The moment he ventured outside the perimeter of the Kong penal colony, the sensors within the chains would have detonated and his skin would have gone up in flames, charring him to ashes within seconds.

But on the day of execution the chains were removed — the only day in a Death Row inmate's life where that was so.

Warden Jallor stepped towards him, careful to keep his distance, his smirk deepening. "Fifteen years ago you swore this day would never come to pass," he said in a mocking tone. "Indeed, how the mighty have fallen."

For the first time in fifteen years, Kerick smiled — a gesture that caused the warden to frown. "Yes," Kerick agreed, his deep rumble of a voice scratchy from a prolonged lack of use, "how the mighty have fallen."

Two guards appeared behind Jallor. The warden made a dismissive motion with his head, indicating it was time to retreat and step aside while the flash-stick was detonated. The warden barely had time to gasp before the flash-stick was snatched from his hand, rendering him completely defenseless from an assault.

"What are you doing?" Jallor snapped at one of the guards, his eyes promising retribution. "Hand the weapon over and take your place at the —"

The warden's words came to a halt when the "guard" holding the flash-stick peeled off his face armor.

Jallor gulped as he looked up into the grim ebony face of Elijah Carter, a Death Row inmate who was scheduled to be executed next week.

Kerick walked slowly towards Jallor. His jaw tightened as he came to a stop before him, staring down at the wide-eyed warden. With a growl he picked Jallor up off of the ground by the neck, his grip tightening until the warden's throat began to elicit gurgling sounds.

"Don't kill him," Elijah warned. "Not yet." He glanced over to the secret panel in the execution pen that allowed for a magistrate of justice to escape should situations like this one ever arise. That panel would take them to the outermost perimeter of Kong. From there, Kerick, Elijah, and Xavier would be on their own in the jungle. "The DNA scanner only responds to living flesh prints, amigo."

"You sure?" Kerick snarled.

"As sure as I can be."

Kerick grunted, but said nothing. He tightened his hold on the warden's neck fractionally, letting Jallor know he'd never allow him to live once they'd gotten from him the palm scan they sought.

"We need the bitch alive," Elijah reminded him.

Nostrils flaring, Kerick turned his head and stared hard at Elijah. Seeing his familiar face, and realizing as he did that Elijah would be executed next week if they were caught, he regained his sanity long enough to let loose of his hold on the sadistic warden.

Jallor gasped when Kerick released his throat. He panted for air as he fell to the ground and turned eyes filled with hatred on the prisoner-turned-executioner.

Kerick smiled slowly, his steel gray eyes locking with the warden's. "Indeed," he murmured, "How the mighty have fallen."

Why an electronic book?

We live in the Information Age—an exciting time in the history of human civilization, in which technology rules supreme and continues to progress in leaps and bounds every minute of every day. For a multitude of reasons, more and more avid literary fans are opting to purchase e-books instead of paper books. The question from those not yet initiated into the world of electronic reading is simply: *Why?*

1. *Price.* An electronic title at Ellora's Cave Publishing and Cerridwen Press runs anywhere from 40% to 75% less than the cover price of the exact same title in paperback format. Why? Basic mathematics and cost. It is less expensive to publish an e-book (no paper and printing, no warehousing and shipping) than it is to publish a paperback, so the savings are passed along to the consumer.

2. *Space.* Running out of room in your house for your books? That is one worry you will never have with electronic books. For a low one-time cost, you can purchase a handheld device specifically designed for e-reading. Many e-readers have large, convenient screens for viewing. Better yet, hundreds of titles can be stored within your new library—on a single microchip. There are a variety of e-readers from different manufacturers. You can also read e-books on your PC or laptop computer. (Please note that Ellora's Cave does not endorse any specific brands.

You can check our websites at www.ellorascave.com or www.cerridwenpress.com for information we make available to new consumers.)

3. *Mobility.* Because your new e-library consists of only a microchip within a small, easily transportable e-reader, your entire cache of books can be taken with you wherever you go.

4. *Personal Viewing Preferences.* Are the words you are currently reading too small? Too large? Too… ANNOYING? Paperback books cannot be modified according to personal preferences, but e-books can.

5. *Instant Gratification.* Is it the middle of the night and all the bookstores near you are closed? Are you tired of waiting days, sometimes weeks, for bookstores to ship the novels you bought? Ellora's Cave Publishing sells instantaneous downloads twenty-four hours a day, seven days a week, every day of the year. Our webstore is never closed. Our e-book delivery system is 100% automated, meaning your order is filled as soon as you pay for it.

Those are a few of the top reasons why electronic books are replacing paperbacks for many avid readers.

As always, Ellora's Cave and Cerridwen Press welcome your questions and comments. We invite you to email us at Comments@ellorascave.com or write to us directly at Ellora's Cave Publishing Inc., 1056 Home Avenue, Akron, OH 44310-3502.

erridwen, the Celtic Goddess of wisdom, was the muse who brought inspiration to story-tellers and those in the creative arts. Cerridwen Press encompasses the best and most innovative stories in all genres of today's fiction. Visit our site and discover the newest titles by talented authors who still get inspired - much like the ancient storytellers did, once upon a time.

CERRIDWEN PRESS

www.cerridwenpress.com